Stars on Fire

Elaine DeBohun

Stars on Fire

Copyright © 2023 by Elaine DeBohun

All rights reserved. No part of this publication may be reproduced, stored in a retrieval system or transmitted in any form by any means, including photocopying, recording, or other electronic or mechanical methods, without the prior written permission by the publisher, except in the case of brief quotations embodied in critical reviews and certain other noncommercial uses permitted by copyright law.

Cover art: John Bingley Garland, 'The Blood Collages' (1791-1875)

This is a work of fiction. Names, characters, places and incidents either are the product of the author's imagination or are used fictitiously, and any resemblance to actual persons, living or dead, businesses, companies, events, or locales is entirely coincidental.

Content warning: This story includes suicidal ideation, graphic war scenes and sexual assault and coercion.

CHARIKLO PRESS

First Edition: May 21, 2o23

ISBN: 9798379120290 (paperback)

Printed in the United States of America

To my King of Wands

"Your soul has fallen to bits and pieces. Good. Rearrange them to suit yourself."

—Herman Hesse, *Steppenwolf*

Prologue

Life is full of regrets. Of things left unsaid that haunt like ghosts and linger in the darkest recesses of the mind.

Move forward, they say. Settle down. Trade the wasteland for a white picket fence, and *whatever you do,* don't look back.

But the pen in my hand whispers louder. *Exhume your dead. Exhume yourself.*

So if you find yourself opening to this page, having stumbled across this written exorcism, I have only one real request: listen closely. What you're about to read, dear reader, is peppered with my deepest secrets. You are my priest, and I am your confessor.

Twins
Paris, December 12, 1918

I traced the thick, symmetrical arch of my brows, leaning closer to the mirror. A pair of effeminate eyes stared back at me—pools of stormy-blue crystal inherited from my grandfather, contained beneath a row of obsidian eyelashes.

Do not forget what you have done, they warned silently.

"Good morning, Narcissus."

I turned to one side, brushing the stubble along my cheekbone. Dane stood in the mirror behind me, sipping from a mug of what I could only assume was wine since we had no running water for coffee.

"For some of us" —I smoothed the left side of my hair, which had been cut around the ears a little too short for my liking— "our face is all we have."

"Out late last night?" he asked.

I glanced down at my watch.

3:47 p.m.

"I got in around ten this morning," I replied, dropping my arm.

"Glad to see you got some rest."

"I wouldn't call it restful. I woke up thinking I was still in the hospital."

Before I could elaborate further, a piece of plaster fell from the ceiling onto my bed, as the sound of a stomping elephant herd rumbled above our heads. Neighbors. We'd been staying in the one-bedroom studio flat at 74 rue du Cardinal Lemoine for almost a month, which was long enough to regret my decision to take the mattress on the floor by the fireplace.

I reached for my pack of cigarettes on the desk, tucking one in my mouth. "I swear," I went on, managing a smile, "they do that every morning like clockwork—and if it's not that, it's someone or other from the dance hall yelling in the stairwell."

"Welcome to the city." Dane glanced to the apartment's sole window overlooking the gutters of the 5th arrondissement. "You get used to the noise."

"I've slept in louder places," I assured, lighting the cigarette.

That was a lie. While I'd originally been excited by the idea of a *Bal Musette* underneath, a blasting accordion all hours of the night felt like an artillery bombardment of its own.

He motioned to my cigarette, giving me a stern look. "Pneumonia is hard enough on the lungs."

I covered my mouth, suppressing the urge to cough. "All the more reason to strengthen them, then." I looked back to the scuffed mirror on the wall and grimaced, as if my physique had dwindled even more in the ten minutes we'd been talking. I was as scrawny as when I'd entered Princeton freshman year—which wasn't actually *that* scrawny—but I'd left the States with such an athletic build that I couldn't help but compare. I frowned, inspecting the stitched flesh under my collarbone. "You don't think this is going to leave a scar…do you?" I turned to him, expectant.

"Well, it's a knife wound. What do you think?"

"I was afraid you'd say that."

Dane snickered to himself, clearly amused by my vanity. "Good thing you got sick and missed the end of the war or you might've ended up with more."

I dragged myself into the kitchen, dunking my hand into the bucket of cold water. "Jeanne likes it. At least one of us does."

"How is the devil these days, anyway?"

"Wouldn't know," I replied, splashing my face.

"You weren't with her last night?"

"I was with Eva." I smirked at him as he leaned against the windowsill with his mug. "I mean Ava. I don't know...she was Italian."

"You didn't give Jeanne a key to the building, then."

"Only if I wanted to tight rope a nightmare of my own making." I turned back to the bucket, allowing the water to trickle down the back of my neck. "I have plenty of those without her help."

"Well, someone who looks remarkably like her just walked in."

"You're funny when you want to be."

"I'm serious," he pressed. "She's coming up the" —Dane paused, interrupted by a knock on the door— "stairwell."

My eyes shot up at him, my face dripping with water. "I'm not here," I whispered.

With a reluctant look, he walked to the door. "Afternoon, Jeanne," he said, cracking it just enough to speak.

"Open up," she demanded.

Dane cleared his throat. "He's not here."

"Like hell he isn't," she countered, pushing past him. Her tawny eyes fell on me as I stood shirtless in the kitchen. "You *lying*—"

"Jeanne," I stammered. "I can explain."

"Where were you last night?" Giving me exactly two seconds to defend myself, she slapped me clear across the face.

"Goddammit, Jeanne!" I followed her to the fireplace. "What the hell are you—how did you get in here?"

"I clean for Jean-Paul downstairs now," she replied, dangling the keys in front of me.

"Oh." I sighed miserably.

"Who was she this time? Hm?" She puckered her perfect lips, her eyes hot with jealousy.

"Has anyone ever told you that you look especially pretty when you're mad?"

"You think you can just call on me whenever you're lonely? Is that it?"

"No..."

"Because I won't always be available, you know. You think you're the only one I invite into my bed?"

"Tell me, do your other suitors satisfy you like I do?" The words spilled out of my mouth, earning me a slap across the opposite cheek. "Fuck, Jeanne! That hurts!" I grabbed her wrists.

"They're certainly less selfish."

I let go of her. "What do you mean by that?"

"I *mean* that you understand the female anatomy about as well as you speak French."

Dane took an awkward sip from his mug, exiling himself with a few steps to the kitchen.

"No need for the hostility, Jeanne." I leaned against the edge of the desk. "How about you give me a chance to make it up to you later?"

She glanced at my mattress on the floor, then cocked her head with a coy smile. "Va te faire foutre."

I pressed my hand to my hot cheek, watching as she closed the door decisively behind her. "She'll be back," I said, turning to Dane.

"What's that saying? Hell hath no fury like a woman scorned? I don't envy you."

I laughed, recounting the drunken spectacle of the night I'd met her downstairs. It had taken me thirty minutes to convince her to come up with me, and it was a wonder we'd even made it to my bed. "It's not nearly that serious."

"For you it's not."

"That wine's gone to your head—she's just looking for solace between the sheets."

Dane shrugged, returning to his post in front of the window. Behind him, the stacked roofs across the street bathed in the orange glow of the afternoon sun.

"So…uh, what did she say?"

His pursed lips were answer enough.

I swiped a shirt from my open suitcase. "Let's go," I urged. "It seems I'm in desperate need of your tutoring."

Dane smiled, grabbing our coats as I opened the front door.

"So, Jeanne's cleaning for Jean-Paul now," he said flatly as we sauntered down the drafty stairwell.

"Who's he got living with him?" I asked, breaking my neck to catch a glimpse of the girl slipping into our neighbor's flat.

"His niece," Dane replied, reaching for the iron-rod door handle.

I grinned puckishly.

"She's young," he said. "Displaced. And with a baby."

"Her circumstance must be dire," I sneered, following him out. "He wouldn't be my first choice to live with."

"And you wouldn't be his, either."

I stopped on the edge of the sidewalk and grabbed another cigarette from my pack, but before I could light it, something scurried across my foot. "What was that?"

Dane looked over his shoulder at me. "What was what?"

Cigarette dangling from my lip, I turned around just in time to see a furry black tail disappear behind a pile of trash. Peeking over the heaps of squaller, I saw that it was a kitten. "What are you doing, moon eyes?" I asked, kneeling down to get a better look.

The kitten stared for a moment before retreating further into its hideaway.

"They're everywhere," said Dane. "If there's one thing Paris isn't lacking, it's cats."

It was a blustery evening, and my coat was pretty thin, but I was still better equipped to handle the cold than my brother.

"When are you going to fix that hole?" I asked, nudging him. "It looks terrible."

He looked down at his shabby attire and the gaping hole in its elbow. "This is my *nice* coat," he said, looking me over. "New shoes?"

"I got them yesterday," I said, excited he'd noticed. "They're called spectator shoes. You don't think they're too flashy, do you?"

"For you? Not at all."

I smirked a bit. "Well, listen—I can patch that hole for you." I shivered, shoving my hands in my pockets. "If you get me a needle and thread."

"Yeah?"

"Yeah, you know…I'm good at that stuff. Me and my golden thread were something of a hot commodity in the trenches."

"I guess those years working with Pop paid off."

"Precisely," I added. "The least I can do is fix your coat for the trouble."

"I told you already—it's no trouble. I'm happy to have you here."

"I know, but I want to. It is winter, after all."

Dane shrugged as we approached the bar. "If you insist." The bustling sounds of thirsty street goers poured out as he opened the door. "No mouthing off this time. I've had enough excitement for one day."

"When have you ever known me to mouth off?"

He only smiled at me slyly as we navigated through the horde to the sticky, wooden bar and took a seat. Then finally, beer in hand, we resumed my French lessons.

I set my sights on the girl I'd noticed when we first walked in, who I'd caught looking down the bar at us more than once. "How do you tell someone they're beautiful?" I asked, admiring how she wore her dusty hair in an off the neck twist.

Dane looked at me flatly. He seemed to be trying his best to avoid her gaze, except when he took a drink and could catch a glimpse over the glass.

"If you're not going to talk to her, I am," I said, turning to him.

"Go ahead."

I tapped on the bar. "I'll be right back."

"Wait," he said, grabbing my arm. "*Tu es moche.*"

I nudged my way into the girl's group of friends, cutting her off from them. "Comment t'appelles-tu?" I asked. Jeanne was right—my French was terrible.

She looked me up and down with her butterfly lashes and grinned, sporting one beauty mark on her left side, just above her lip. "Camille...and who do I have the pleasure?"

"You're English."

"Half English, moitié français—and you're American, are you not?"

"I am. Did my accent give me away?" Taking her smile as confirmation, I offered her my hand. "I'm Holden."

"Very nice to meet you."

"The pleasure is all mine." I brought her palm to my lips for a kiss. "Tu es moche."

"*What?*"

I shot a look down the bar to Dane, who was quick to turn away. "Oh no—I—" I whipped around to Camille. "I don't think that's what I meant to say to you."

She could hardly talk, she was laughing so hard. "You don't speak French, do you?" she asked.

"I'm ashamed to admit that I don't," I replied. "That's what I get for trying to show off."

"Well, what were you trying to say?"

I tilted my head with a confident grin.

"Dane, this is Camille," I said, leading her over to our corner spot. "Camille, Dane."

Maneuvering her way to the bar, she squeezed in between us. "What brings the two of you to Paris?"

"The war for me," I replied. "But Dane's lived here on and off for years."

"How interesting," she said, turning to him. "Where do you live now?"

"Rue de Cardinale Lemoine."

"Your accent is good. Parlez-vous français?"

"Oui."

She nodded slowly, amusement again washing over her. "So, *you're* the one who told him to call me ugly."

Feeling vindicated, I sipped my beer as his face turned red as a beet.

"I don't think that at all, just so we're clear," he stammered.

She beamed with her smiley eyes, looking satisfied. "Merci, Dane."

"He speaks Italian, too," I added. "He's a real linguist."

"And you, Holden?"

"Ich spreche Deutsch."

"I see," she murmured, looking intrigued. German was hardly a romance language.

"What about you?" Dane asked. "Habitez-vous ici?"

"My father owns a marina here," she replied, taking a sip of his beer. "I used to live in between, but Paris was certainly a better place to be than London during the war, don't you think?"

A mere twenty years old, she was an enchanting mix of charming and lively—marriage material—the kind of girl that twirled her hair in between her fingers when she listened to you talk. I could tell Dane was just as flustered by her as I was. But something about the way she smiled so hard with her teeth made my vacant heart skip a beat, and I could tell she liked me by the way her arm kept brushing up against mine.

Finally, I leaned in and asked, "What are you doing tomorrow, Camille?"

"Well!" She clapped her hands together. "A very nice gentleman has asked me on a date, so I suppose I'll do whatever he has planned."

I lowered my voice, softening my eyes. "Tell him you can't go because you're going out with me instead."

She smiled, seating her chin in her palm. "On one condition."

"Anything."

"What's my birthday?"

I cocked an eyebrow at her. "Sorry?"

"If you can guess my birthday, I'll go out with you."

"You're kidding."

"You have a 1 in 365 chance." She glanced at Dane with a mischievous smirk. "You have three guesses."

I'll admit, this was a first.

"I don't know," I said, throwing up a hand in defeat. "June 17th."

Her smile dropped, and her brow wrinkled. "What?" she asked, looking back at her friends down the bar. "How did you know that?"

"Wasn't this whole thing a little unnecessary if you were just going to let me win?" I teased.

"What made you say June 17th?"

"June 17th is *my* birthday—I wasn't being serious."

She turned to Dane, gaping. "That's not really his birthday."

"No, it is. June 17, 1894."

Camille and I locked eyes with each other, simultaneously about to speak, then waiting for the other to do so.

"I suppose that makes us twins," she said finally.

"Are you a woman of your word?"

"I am."

"So then," I replied, smug. "It's a date."

Her grin was playful but her words were sharp. "I would *never* go on a date with a man who called me ugly."

The busy rue had mellowed by the time I finally walked out of the bar and into the cold, with Dane by my side and Camille's address in my pocket.

"Hey—home's *this* way," Dane reminded.

"I'm not going home."

"You do it to yourself," he called after me.

I turned around and shrugged, grinning ear to ear as I left him behind. It only took a short walk and a single knock for Jeanne to answer her door. Looking satisfied, she leaned in the doorway seductively.

"I'm lonely," I admitted.

"And here you are."

"Here I am."

We held eye contact for a few moments before she fell into me, wrapping her arms around my neck. "You're freezing."

"Can I come in?"

"That depends," she teased, lightly brushing my nose with hers. "Are you sorry?"

I'd hardly murmured *yes* before our lips locked, and she pulled me straight through the door.

How American
Paris, December 13, 1918

I COULD HAVE THANKED Jeanne for the good night's sleep if I'd stayed long enough to do so. Instead, I slid out the door undetected while she was still dreaming.

I had some time to kill before I picked Camille up for our Sunday stroll, so I set out into the chilly fog toward Montparnasse, hoping to pick up some thread for Dane's coat. I couldn't help but compare myself to everyone I passed along the way—women in their oversized collars, men in their Mackinaw jackets. Since arriving in Paris, I'd updated my own wardrobe enough to fit in, but I still felt like an outsider, viewing civilian life from behind a glass. Shops felt alien, and errands felt pointless. Once faced with the constant threat of death, everything else fell flat. What was it like for the rest of them, to go about their window shopping without the whispers of the dead in their ear?

I scanned the streets for my brother—set up with his easel and supplies—until I finally located him on a café corner, fully absorbed in an oil painting.

"Looking good," I said.

"Oh." He turned around with a startled expression. "I didn't hear you walk up."

"Let me see."

He swayed to the left, revealing the scene of two women in obscenely large hats.

"I wonder what they're talking about," I mused, studying the portrait.

"What brings you out this way?"

"Just taking in the city," I replied, posting up on the limestone building to his side. "Being that you're out here every Sunday, I thought I'd see what the fuss was about."

"I figured you'd be sleeping in or something."

"I don't kiss and tell."

He glanced over his shoulder to see me smirking. "*Right.* Your moral compass forbids you."

"I'm supposed to meet up with Camille around three...I'm hoping the sun comes out and burns off this fog." I looked Dane up and down, assessing the thin, paint-stained overcoat he wore. "I stopped for thread so I can patch that hole before I go back out."

"Thanks," he replied, steadying his chapped fingers. "My coat should be next to the desk."

"Will do. It'll put Marie Antoinette to shame by the time I'm done with it."

"Have you decided where you're taking Camille yet?"

I glanced across the street with a lighthearted laugh. "Call me predictable, but..."

What happened next—the only witness is my own shaky recollection.

"BACK UP!" someone shouted. "I mean it—give him some air!"

On the ground in tremors, I scanned the slew of people surrounding me for a familiar face. A tether back to this world.

"Do you know where you are, buddy?"

My eyes darted to the black man who'd appeared at my side, then to Dane, kneeling next to him, then to the rest of my observers. Dane looked at me expectantly, but I was too frightened to speak.

"Where'd you go?"

I turned to the stranger. His soulful obsidian eyes told me he knew all too well. "St. Quentin," I whispered.

"You want a cigarette?"

I managed a nod, and he reached into his trouser pocket, pulling out a pack and promptly placing one in my mouth, lighting it for me.

"Get back! Nothing to see here," he yelled over his shoulder at the remaining gawkers.

I grabbed the cigarette, scooting up into a sitting position against the wall. "What happened?" I asked.

"A car backfired," Dane replied.

"Any loud noise is enough to set it off," the man added. "The shellshock."

The word was enough to send a shiver down my spine. I shook my head in defense. "I was hospitalized for influenza. I haven't been right since the fever."

"You have nightmares?"

I took a nervous puff of the cigarette. "Everyone has nightmares," I mumbled. "Can I get a hand?"

"Grab on," said Dane.

I clenched the cigarette between my teeth as I dusted off my pants. "You're American," I noted, tilting my chin at the magnificently tall stranger who'd come to my aid. "AEF?"

"Shell got me good in my leg—been here since September." He dropped his eyes to his feet, then lifted them to me. "You?"

"I was a captain with the 108th," I replied. "Company E, 2nd battalion."

He was quick to give me a salute. "Private Eldred Carter, 369th infantry, at your service."

"New York," I said, extending my hand instead. "Me, too."

"Harlem." A broad, sunny smile stretched across his face as he took hold.

"Thank you," I added, embarrassed. "For the help."

"Hey—"

My eyes shot up at him.

"Not half of them have seen what you've seen. What *we've* seen," he said, releasing me. "Now you take care of yourself, Captain. You hear?"

I nodded to myself, rotating the cigarette with my tongue. I could feel Dane waiting for me to speak as the good Samaritan walked away, but all I could think about was getting inside. "I need to go home and wash up," I said.

"Are you okay?"

"Fine," I promised. "We'll catch up later."

I inhaled three more cigarettes on the short walk home. As badly as I wanted to deny it, I knew as well as Eldred Carter that I had shellshock. I'd seen it in my men—I knew what it looked like. It's not like I hadn't noticed my ever-worsening insomnia, or that I could never keep still. I had the nightmares, the mood swings—and now, the flashbacks. I was alive, sure, but only for my prospective freedom to be tainted. It was a sick kind of purgatory, really.

I was in a bad state by the time I reached our flat, thinking it would've been better to have never left the battlefield. I imagined hustling up the stairwell and locking the door behind me, spilling the contents of my suitcase in search of my 1911 Colt, which would mold to my hand like an old familiar. But I was slowed when a rustling caught my attention, and I turned from the halfway opened door to see a pair of glowing eyes peeking out at me from the trash pile. "You again," I mumbled.

Continuing inside and out of the cold, my fingers slipped on the iron door handle, causing it to slam behind me. I mouthed apologies to the youthful girl standing outside of Jean-Paul's apartment, smiling cheekily as she balanced a bag of groceries in one arm and a bundled baby in the other.

"Let me help you with those," I insisted, relieving her of the bag.

"Merci."

"You're Jean-Paul's niece?" I asked, waiting as she searched her pockets for the key.

"Jean-Paul, oui." She smiled again, lifting her gaze from the baby to me. Her eyes, seemingly untouched by sorrow, shimmered. "Est-ce que je peux?"

I nodded along, uncertain of what I was agreeing to. She motioned for me to take the baby.

"*Oh*—okay," I said, setting the groceries against the wall.

"Merci beaucoup," she said, delicately passing him off to me.

She turned her attention back to the task of finding her keys, and I turned mine to the baby in my arms, who'd readjusted himself, snuggly against my chest. Enamored by the sleepy, tranquil eyes staring back at me, I thought of sitting around the campfire in Ypres, the light of the fire illuminating the photograph of a child about the same age.

"*Henri.*"

Tucking the blanket under his chin, I whispered to myself. "Henri."

"Je m'appelle Meg," she added.

"Holden," I replied.

"*Margaret!* Est-ce vous?"

As if she'd been caught past curfew, she grinned guiltily with flushing cheeks, insinuating that I'd better go.

"*Margaret?*"

"Here you go," I said, handing the baby back.

Hearing the footsteps of Jean-Paul on the other side of the door, I slipped around the corner of the staircase, disappearing just in time for him to collect her.

I unlocked the apartment door and glanced down at my watch. I had three hours before I was supposed to meet Camille. I turned to the mirror on the wall, to my twin in the reflection. My shadow I couldn't outrun.

Unlatching my suitcase, I rummaged through the layers of clothing, eventually pulling the pistol from its hibernation. Beneath it, the box that housed my Distinguished Service Cross, which I hadn't opened since I left the hospital. Laying the gun across my lap, I glanced to the door. One good shot to the head is all it would take. One good, *loud* shot. I thought of the girl downstairs with her baby. Surely, she would hear it.

I couldn't possibly.

I picked up the box and opened it, setting the pistol aside. Alongside the glimmering medals sat Rick Spofford's sooty, gold necklace. Untangling the delicate chain gracefully, I let the pendant sit in my palm for a moment before pocketing it.

Settling at the desk, I laid Dane's coat over my lap. I'd cut a few patches from an old tunic the day before—and carefully threading the needle, I started stitching them onto one elbow at a time. My hands moved quickly, only stopping to rethread when it wasn't perfect.

In and out, in and out, one stitch, two.

I'd spent almost two years at my family's tailoring shop, working to earn my keep of tuition for Princeton. I could've easily followed in my father's footsteps and taken up the trade, avoiding this whole mess entirely. But as he would say, that wasn't *God's plan*. Such a remark might've eased Rick's mind, but not mine. There wasn't much that would ease mine.

By the time I was finished with the coat, it looked not only warmer, but damn stylish, and I laid it across Dane's bed for him to find—clear evidence I'd been there. Quickly, I threw on a nicer tweed sport coat and dipped my hand in the bucket of water, running it through my hair. Slipping the Colt into my coat pocket, I turned to what was left of our measly rations in the kitchen. There wasn't much in the ice box in terms of food, but there *was* a spot of milk, which I poured into a small cracked tea saucer.

The kitten was still cowering in the same spot when I returned, and I knelt and called to it, scooting my offering across the ground. "You must be hungry," I whispered, rising to my feet.

. . .

Camille was dressed in a royal blue coat with a mink collar, radiating enough sunshine to offset the dreary day when the cab pulled up outside her boxwood-lined gate. "*Nice neighborhood*," I murmured under my breath, trying my best not to gawk at the lavish estate house behind her.

"You came!" she exclaimed as I opened the cab door.

"You thought I wouldn't show?"

"You're ten minutes late."

"Were you counting?"

She narrowed her eyes at me with a smile as I stepped out of the car and offered her my arm.

"Where are we going?" she asked.

I shot her a flirtatious grin, climbing into the backseat next to her. "You'll have to wait and see."

Camille sighed, leaning back on my lap as the driver pulled onto the street. She gazed upward at me with a smile, as if it were the most natural thing she could ever do—as if we'd known each other since we were children and had grown up capturing fireflies and playing hide and seek together.

"What?" she asked.

Amused, I reached for the piece of hair that had caught in her eyelash, brushing it away before lowering my voice. "I didn't expect you would be so forward."

"You think this is forward? You shouldn't assume."

I smiled sheepishly. "My apologies, then."

"What's that in your pocket?" she asked, turning her cheek on my lap. "It feels heavy."

"Uh—" I shifted the left side of my coat.

She dropped her jaw, widening her eyes for dramatic display. "You brought a *gun* on our date?"

"So, it's a date, then?"

She grinned, her eyes gleaming up at me. In the light I could see that they weren't brown, but more of a hazel with a golden ring. "A soldier through and through," she remarked. "How has your day been so far?"

"It just became great."
"It wasn't good before?"
"It was fine."
"Did you have any more French lessons with your brother?"
"No." I chuckled. "I think it's probably best I shelve that dream."
"If you're fluent in one language, you're more likely to become fluent in another. Maybe it's just that you need a better teacher—" Interrupted by the driver slamming on the breaks, Camille slid partway off my lap, catching herself on my knee. She sat up swiftly, a mess of tousled hair, and I looked her dead in the eye, wearing my most ambiguous smirk.
"You want to teach me French?" I asked.
She only had time to blink in response—dazed by the abruptness of our arrival or my boldness. Maybe both.
"Champ de Mars, Monsieur," said the driver, cutting through our chemistry with one glance to the back seat.
I stepped out of the taxi in full view of the Eiffel tower, reaching around to offer Camille my hand. "What?" I asked, noting her grin as she took hold. *"How American of him,"* I mimicked playfully. "That's what you're thinking, aren't you?"
"I might be." She laughed, grabbing onto my arm as we made our way to the grassy plain, passing underneath the tower. "How long have you been in Paris?"
"Long enough for it to make an impression." I smiled at her. The park was busier than I'd anticipated for such a cold, damp day and every leisurely sound had me glancing over my shoulder.
"And where is home?"
"Virginia," I replied, turning back to her.
"And your family? What are they like?"
"Well, there's Dane...I've got a younger brother and sister: Marcie and Jamie—" I flinched at the pop of a nearby picnicker opening a bottle of champagne. "His name is James, but we call him Jamie."

Jesus Christ, keep it together.

"Hey," she cooed, sliding her fingers down my arm until her hand was cupped in mine. "You seem tense. Are you all right?"

Having flirted with the prospect of ending it all just a few hours prior, I was admittedly far from it. The fear of losing control again was too loud to ignore, but I couldn't tell her that. "Just a little overstimulated," I admitted.

"Well, why don't we walk this way?" She led me away from the crowds, toward a group of loitering pigeons.

"What are you doing?"

Camille pulled a small bag of seed from her purse. "Here," she directed, reaching for my hands.

I indulged her, feeling the collective attention of the flock fall on me as she poured the seed into my palm.

"You have nice hands," she gushed, closing my fingers. "What did you do before the war?"

"Well, before the war—I was in school."

"Oh?" she asked, flinging seed. The birds gathered at our feet, flapping their wings. "Studying what?"

"I—" I laughed, watching her eyes widen in delight as a pigeon landed on my shoulder. "I was studying writing," I went on, lifting my palm to its beak. "I was a year from finishing my degree when I enlisted."

"What were you running from, then?"

I must have turned white as a ghost.

"I'm only teasing. Would you ever go back and finish it? Your degree?"

"I don't think so," I replied, glad to move on. "A good writer is like a magician…he's able to extract medicine from poison with words alone." I shrugged. "I think you're either born with it or you're not."

She smiled, knitting her brow. "And where do you fall on that spectrum?"

"Let's just say I was a better tailor."

"A tailor!"

I clenched up, feeling a tug on my hair. "Ah—"

Camille erupted in laughter, lunging through the horde to my rescue. "Shoo!" she said, waving her hand.

"Is that so unbelievable?" I asked as the pair of birds flew to the ground. "That I was a tailor?"

"Hmmm." She eyed me inquisitively, before at last deciding on her answer. "Holden the tailor. I can see it."

"I worked as one in my father's shop for a few years. See, we have this—" I paused, suddenly self-conscious. "Sorry. I feel like I've been talking about myself this whole time."

She giggled as a pigeon landed on her shoulder, and I reached over, removing the fluffy bird with both hands. "What about you?" I asked nervously, holding the pigeon so she could pet it.

"I'm in the culinary arts. Pastries, specifically."

"Really?"

"Is that so unbelievable?" she teased, running her fingers across its gray feathers.

"Not in the slightest."

I released the pigeon and followed Camille over to the nearest bench, taking a seat next to her. "Why all the questions?" I asked, wrapping my arm around the back.

"Isn't that how you get to know someone?"

I could feel my expression go sideways, as if I'd forgotten that the point of courting was to form a relationship, not immediately jump into bed together. I was as novice as they come.

"I'm not so sure you'd like what you found." I turned forward, scanning the lawn. "If you really got to know me."

"Why wouldn't I like you?"

I paused, motioning to a couple canoodling on the bench directly across from us. "See those people?" Camille nodded, leaning in. "He doesn't have a care in the world and neither does she." I pointed to another group of onlookers admiring the tower. "And them—all they care about is the view."

"What's wrong with that?"

"Nothing." I shrugged. "But the ability to live in the present is a luxury. Not everyone is so lucky." I pursed my lips and turned away. "I guess I'm a bit of a cynic. It comes out sometimes. Always at the worst times."

"It's all right to break character every now and then."

"What you mean to say is that I was much more fun last night," I joked.

She softened her tone. "I only mean to say it's okay to be yourself. Whoever he is."

"You thought last night was an act?"

"Just that it seemed like you've done it a hundred times."

My eyes found the ground, not wanting to tell her I had.

"Did you feel that?"

I glanced up to see her squinting to the sky.

"It's raining," she added.

I held out my palm. "Just sprinkling."

No sooner had I said the words than the drizzle picked up its frequency—not enough to run for cover, but enough to dampen the mood. Camille grimaced, holding her hands over her head as if to protect her hair from the incoming moisture, and seizing the opportunity, I tore off my coat and held it up over us. "Better?"

"Oh—*much.*"

"So," I prodded, "why did you talk to me if you thought I was playing a part?"

"I don't know." She grinned, holding up her side of the shelter with one hand. "I suppose I saw a light in you."

The sentiment took me back to childhood, when Marcie would scream at the sight of a spider, and I'd rush to the rescue—of the spider, that is—releasing it outside before anyone could squash it, and the adults would say, *such a light, you are, Holden.* It might've been true once.

"How do you figure?" I asked, inching closer to her.

"It's in the eyes," she whispered, brushing my cheek with her pointer finger.

I drew back to look at her as the raindrop percussion beat on the coat above our heads. "I'd really like to kiss you."

"Would you?"

I closed my eyes, bringing my mouth to hers. Lips as soft as a rosebud. A kiss so perfect I didn't dare do it again.

It was dark when the taxi pulled up outside her front gate, with us snuggled perfectly together in the back. I'd divulged more about myself to her in one afternoon than anyone else in the entirety of my Paris stay. Her company was a balm to my scorched soul—a prospect that both comforted and terrified me.

"It's a nice night," I remarked, gazing up as I helped her out. "Great for stargazing."

"Funny how the fog lifted for the moon and not the sun, don't you think?" she asked as I accompanied her up the stone walkway. We walked past the hibernating landscaping, veiled in winter darkness, at last finding our profiles illuminated by the sconces alongside her portico.

"I had a really nice time with you today," I said.

"Likewise." Camille leaned back on the front door, opening it slightly, tempting me to make my move. "I suppose the fates know what they're doing from time to time."

"So, I guess this is…"

"Muffin! No!" she shouted, her attention seized by the dog that had dashed through the partially open door.

I whipped around to see a tan Pomeranian with a white collar, staring back at us defiantly from the edge of the yard.

"Come here," Camille demanded, stomping her foot on the stair's edge. The dog lunged, as if she were threatening to run away, and Camille groaned. "I swear she lives to make my life miserable."

"I got her," I said. "I love dogs."

"She's not a dog. She's a little monster, Holden—she'll take your finger off if you try and touch her!"

I crept down the stairs, stepping over the boxwood. "Aw…" I lowered my voice, making a kissing noise. "You're a *vicious* girl, aren't you?"

The fleecy demon bared her fangs, and I turned back to see Camille peeking through her fingers, anticipating bloodshed.

"Let's go, Muffin," I said, scooping her from underneath. I stepped back over the boxwood, holding the dog in one arm as I walked back to Camille, who looked as if she'd just witnessed Moses' parting of the Red Sea.

"I can't believe it."

"No?"

"You don't understand. Muffin hates everyone but my mother."

As if on cue, the dog snarled, lifting her lips so we could see her teeth. "I know," I cooed, meeting her stunned, beady eyes. "So *scary*."

Camille opened the door, allowing me to drop Muffin inside.

"She's cute," I snickered.

"She's an absolute nightmare." Camille laughed, adjusting her leg to prevent another escape.

"My grandad had a grumpy old German Spitz."

"My word, you really have a way with animals, don't you?"

"How can someone not love animals? They're inherently good. Even Muffin."

"You don't think people can be inherently good?"

"Maybe some."

She smiled sweetly, retreating behind the door.

"Wait," I said, preventing her from closing it completely. "Can I see you again?"

Camille eyed me through the crack, mirroring me as I leaned in. "Yes," she said, opening the door just enough so she could peck me on the lips.

THE RECKONER
YPRES, BELGIUM, AUGUST 1918

CHARLIE BECKHAM GROANED, glaring disdainfully at the can of Maconochie stew in his hand. "This stuff is a mystery even to the Brits who can it."

"Their rations are a mystery," said Rick Spofford. "With their tea instead of coffee."

"I feel sick enough as it is without adding this lard on top," Beck replied, setting the can down and scooting it away with his foot. He slumped his shoulders, eyeing the can like a picky child.

Connor Mullins sat to his left, fixating his dark eyes on the fire. "It's not so bad warmed up," he added. The scrawny sergeant needed the fat more than Beckham, that was for sure.

Rick glanced upward, scraping the inside of his own aluminum can. "You'd better eat it anyway," he said to Beck. "Just don't think about it."

"Gee, Spof, wish I'd have thought of that!"

"God…" Mullins sighed. "I'd love a cup of coffee."

I narrowed my eyes on Beckham's can, flicking my pocketknife to the ground an inch away from it.

"Can you stop doing that?" he pleaded. "Makes me nervous."

Managing a grin, I ran my finger absently over the hardcover German novel sitting in my lap.

"You're quiet," said Rick, returning my knife.

I fanned the worn edges of the book leisurely with my thumb. "Just trying to get lost in someone else's story for a while."

"I saw you take it off one of the gunners. Is it any good?"

"*Die Leiden des jungen Werthers.*" I lifted my eyes to our gentle giant, feeling the soreness of my gashed eyebrow. "It's a story of unrequited love," I said, flipping through. "I've read it once before."

Whatever Rick was going to say, he swallowed his words at the sight of a photo bookmarking the pages of the latter half.

"I guess this was as far as he got," I murmured, picking it up gingerly. Holding it up to the light for a closer look, we studied silently the portrait of a baby, no older than a year. I reached up for my copper penny necklace, only to remember it wasn't there.

Beckham, sitting directly across from me, placed a fourth cigarette between his lips. "What's that?" he asked.

"Nothing." I tucked the photo safely within the bound pages, figuring I'd save him the trouble. It was easier not to think that the enemy soldier was a living, breathing person whose children would be missing them. "Spare a cigarette, Beck?"

"Sure thing." He took another out of the box, lighting it with the cherry of his own before handing it off to me.

I took a drag and looked above to the empty sky and to the cinders which burned off and floated upward. I could feel Victor Thelander studying my every move from his seat adjacent to me, while Eric Pitman slouched next to him in a dead sleep. The kids of our ragtag group, barely nineteen.

"*Shit,*" said Mullins, gazing upward. "Damn star is blazing brighter than Hell itself."

"It's not a star," Beckham sneered. "That's an insult to Jupiter."

"It's Mars," I corrected, flicking my ash.

"Either way," replied Beckham. "It's *not* a star."

"Mars is always the easiest to spot because of the red color," I added.

"Listen to the expert."

"I'm hardly an expert," I argued. "It was just the first thing my brother taught me as a kid. We used to stargaze up on our parents' roof."

"I wish I had a brother," Beckham muttered. "Or even a sister."

"You're an only child?" Mullins teased. "I would've never guessed."

Beckham shot him a glare, then rolled his eyes.

"My brother died when I was three. I don't remember him much."

We turned to Thelander, who'd been quiet up until that point.

"Tuberculosis," he added.

Rick sighed. "Sorry to hear that, kid."

"Have you ever heard the story of Castor and Pollux, Thelander?" I asked.

His eyes perked up from under his helmet. "No, Lieutenant."

"The expert," Beckham mocked.

Paying him no mind, I leaned my elbows on my knees, holding the novel tightly in both hands. "In Greek mythology, there was a pair of twin brothers—one mortal and the other a demigod."

"How did that work?" asked Beck.

"Shhhhh."

"You don't want to know," I replied, smug. "Anyway, they were so close that when the mortal brother died in battle, the demigod offered to split his immortality with him."

Rick cleared his throat. "That's what makes it a myth."

"Right." I kept my eyes on the faint smile of the kid. "But if it were bound in a book, we might call it truth."

"Here we go," Mullins groaned.

"Because it's God alone that determines our fate," Rick countered.

"Have you ever stopped to think that fate and free will aren't mutually exclusive?"

"It's not my place to question Him and look to the stars for answers."

"Well, why not?" I shot back. "If God governs everything, that would include the heavenly bodies, would it not?"

"Hey!"

"*What*, Beck?" I snapped.

"I was asking a serious question—how was one a demigod and the other a mortal if they were twins?"

"One was fathered by a God and the other by a king."

Beckham shrugged, seeming satisfied.

"At least I think that's how it went. Dane tells it much better than I do," I added.

"Do you and your brother have different fathers, too?" asked Thelander.

"Different mothers. You'd never be able to tell, though."

"Why's that?" asked Rick.

"I'm the only one with dark hair. If anything, I'm the one that sticks out." I smiled to myself. "If I hadn't been eavesdropping on him and our pop talking, I would've never known."

That wasn't completely true. There had always been something—or rather, a lack of something between Dane and my mother—as if she knew that for all her trying, she could never take the place of Celia, our father's first wife. Still, for my seven-year-old self, it was hard to hear that we were only *half* brothers, as if the word in front somehow watered down the blood shared between us.

Rick pushed his blond hair, thick with dirt and grime, back. "Well, I was lucky enough to be born with three sisters."

I turned to him. "You've never told me that."

"Because I wouldn't let you near a single one of them."

This coaxed a few laughs from Beckham and Mullins, who exchanged knowing looks.

"What?"

I must've looked offended, because Beck was quick to backtrack. "Sorry! It's just...well, you know."

"We all saw you with that redhead in Voormezele," Mullins added.

I thought about playing dumb, but what did it matter now if they knew now?

"Crucify me. You'd all do the same thing if given the chance." I paused, cocking my head toward Rick. "Except the priest, over here."

"Not me," said Beckham. "I'm happy as a clam."

Mullins snickered. "For good reason."

"Hey—" His muddy hazel eyes expanded. "Don't talk about Dora around the campfire…come on! She's off limits!"

"Then don't show us her picture!"

"I would do the same thing if I had the chance," admitted Pitman, finally joining the land of the living.

"No one has a chance in hell as long as *he's* around," Beckham added. "All he has to do is look at them and they fall under some sort of spell." He turned to Mullins. "I've seen him do it."

I frowned defensively. "He's exaggerating."

"Is he, Thom?"

I turned to see Rick grinning at me, but I had trouble returning his smile. We'd all heard the shelling. The thought of the Flemish farmgirl—the ecstasy I'd shared with her—pinned beneath a pile of rubble made my chest ache. If anyone had been under a spell, it was me.

"God will watch over her," he added softly.

"I can't imagine the damage he could do to an artillery shell, Rick."

The banter around the barrel fire went out like a snuffed candle wick, and a grim silence took over, as if we'd just remembered where we were. Lacing my fingers, I turned back to face the flames.

"This the 108th?"

I looked up to greet the unknown voice, belonging to one of three men standing in the shadows behind Pitman and Thelander.

"That's us," said Thelander, looking over his shoulder.

"Which one of you is Lieutenant Thompson?"

The boys exchanged a series of glances, all of them waiting for me to speak up.

"Who's asking?" I said, stubbing my cigarette on the trench wall.

"Captain Cary Olsen, Company K."

I rose to my feet, but he held out his hand as he walked further into the light, revealing his face. "At ease, Lieutenant."

I took my seat. "Sir," I stuttered, "who's looking for me?"

"Everybody."

Unnerved, I watched as he took his time unfolding a piece of paper.

"The 108th infantry set precedent in capturing the trenches along York Road today," he read out loud. "The unit was led by a young lieutenant named Thompson, carrying a shotgun." His eyes darted up to me. "I take it that's you, Lieutenant?"

The collective attention of the campfire fell on me, and I looked across the fire smoke to Beckham. "Yes sir," I replied. "That was me."

"And who do you think you are to lead a charge against orders?"

"We had no acting commander, sir," Beck interjected. "If it weren't for him—"

Olsen raised his hand.

"Our captain was shot within the first hour," I said.

"You were told to wait for reinforcements."

"The reinforcements took too long. Sir."

He lowered the letter. "You led a suicide mission with thirty men."

"Twenty-six," Rick murmured, glancing up at the captain. "There were twenty-six of us."

"Men from the 105th left their post to join up with you."

"All due respect, Captain," I replied. "No one likes being a sitting duck."

"And no one likes a maverick who thinks he's smarter than his superiors."

"Sir, it was by no means an attempt to distinguish myself," I countered. "I never intended to lead a single person anywhere."

EARLIER THAT DAY———————

Counting my breaths, I leaned back against the battered dirt, watching as the smoke crept across the top of our foxhole. The absence of my copper penny rested like a crater in my chest, a reminder of the poisonous savagery that seeps into the minds of men at war. It was all that my grandfather had hoped my generation would avoid, yet here I was. In the wasteland.

"How long are they going to make us wait here?" Beckham whispered sharply. "Until a shell takes us out?"

To my right, the glassy eyes of Captain Bowen slid past me, blood dripping between their lashes and falling peacefully onto his cheek. I grabbed the whistle from around his neck. "Hell with this," I spat, situating it between my teeth. "Beck, give me your shotgun."

He slid his sergeant's issued trench gun across the dirt. "What are you doing?"

I pumped it, peering over the edge of the hole at the German line twenty yards away. "While they take their goddamned time having a tea party, *I'm* going to figure out how to get us out of here."

"Are you insane?"

"The sooner someone captures this trench, the sooner it'll be done."

Rick leaned in. "There's some infantry in a foxhole by the fence line—if we can make it there, we can pick up what's left of them."

"Take Mullins with you on the right side. Thelander, Pitman" —I glanced at the pair of lanky privates who'd joined us in the hole— "follow Spofford, and keep your heads down. Beck, are you with me?"

Beckham cocked his pistol with jittery hands. "If I die, you better write Dora and tell her it was your fault."

Rick kissed his pendant of Saint Stephen before tucking it back into his collar. "Ready when you are, Thom," he said.

"One." I exhaled. *"Two—"* Throwing the shotgun over my shoulder, I hopped the top of the dugout into the line of fire, emptying my lungs into an ear-splitting whistle.

Beckham and I yielded left as we charged ahead, diving head on into the dirt. A few others joined us on the ground as we fired back at the enemy gunners—him with his pistol, and me with my shotgun. I looked right to see Rick in the neighboring foxhole, waiting with Mullins and the rest of the guys they'd picked up.

"I can see you in my scope, American," a thick German accent barked. "The blind leading the blind!"

"Wir sehen uns in einer Minute," I taunted back.

Clutching the smoking hole in his chest, he fell to the ground and another gunner took over, sending a bullet between Beckham and me.

"Cover me," I said, taking aim at the second gunner.

"Wha? You can't be—it'll take them less than a minute to get there!"

"Just do it, Beck!"

"All right! All right," he muttered back. "You crazy sonofabitch."

I held my breath, steadying my aim. *"Auf Wiedersehen,"* I whispered, taking the shot.

In a state of possession, I held down the trigger, pumping the shotgun three, four, five times continuously as I rushed toward the unmanned station. A faint cheering erupted from the field. I jumped into the trench, pulled down in a stronghold by an arm around my neck. A gunner held me from behind as another pointed his rifle, but I squirmed enough to make him fumble his aim and shoot his mate. He hurled back, slamming the butt of his gun into my head.

When I opened my eyes, it was to the sound of a cocked trigger. "This is only to tease you," warned a voice, pressing the pistol into my temple.

This was it. I'd die a slow, excruciating death in a prison camp. Wasted potential, like the rest of my life. Then, as if divine intervention were tempting me to believe, an American platoon appeared out of thin air, showering me in the German's blood.

Pushing him off, I stumbled to my feet, scanning the slumped bodies leaning haphazardly over each other.

"Company E— who's in charge?" shouted a 105th captain from the top of the trench.

I wiped the blood from my face, lifting my eyes to the sun. "No one."

"Well, who are you?"

"Lieutenant Holden Thompson, sir."

Olsen turned to the campfire, nodding subtly. "You lied to recruiters in New York about your schooling so you could enlist as a private," he said.

I could see a wave of curiosity flicker over the faces of Mullins, Pitman and Thelander.

"Isn't that right?"

I dropped my voice to a murmur. "Yes sir."

"I also know that you tried to refuse lieutenant when you arrived in France." He paused, clasping his hands behind his back. "You see, Lieutenant. The best leaders never intend to lead."

I glanced over at Rick, confused.

"As of today, you're acting captain for Company E." He must've sensed my hesitation, because he was quick to clarify that the promotion wasn't up for debate. "General O'Ryan's orders."

"Yes sir."

"See you tomorrow, Captain."

I fiddled with the end of my cigarette butt solemnly, listening to the sound of their boots shuffle across the floorboards.

"I sure wouldn't want to be on the other end of *the Reckoner's* gun barrel."

I glanced up and over Thelander's head to see that one of Olsen's lieutenants had lagged behind. "The Reckoner?"

He adjusted his rifle over his shoulder, grinning like a shot fox. "That's what the 105th is calling you."

Make A Wish
Paris, December 13, 1918 cont.

The kitten was hiding when I got back to our flat, but I could see that the saucer was empty, which brought a smile to my face. My afternoon with Camille had been the perfect distraction from my problems, but the existential dread had returned with a vengeance, and I found myself already needing another. Lucky for me, the *Bal Musette* on the first floor was in full swing.

I lost myself in the blasting accordion music as I walked through the door and through the tangle of conversations, making my way to the bar. I ordered one beer, then two, then four—quickly finding myself subdued with a homesickness for nothing or no one in particular in the sweaty, crowded dance hall.

"*Edie!*"

I was roused from my sulking by a screech in my ear, then, a foxy blonde, carelessly bumping into my shoulder. "Oh—sorry hun," slurred the American girl, turning to make sure her girlfriend was still following.

I watched her bounce through the crowd, admiring her figure from my seat. I could tell by the way she held her chin that she could probably drink me under the table, and if I really hated myself, I would've gone over and talked to her. But from the look of it, she'd found another expat to dote on her anyway. I did a double take at the dirty blond whose arm she was hanging on. At first glance, he could've been mistaken for Rick, whose pendant necklace still sat in the bottom of my pants pocket. In another life, maybe it could have been him.

I paid my tab and stumbled out the door into the dark, almost tripping over my new friend in the process. *"Jesus,"* I scolded. The kitten bolted, obviously spooked, and I followed, searching the mounds of garbage. "Hey…I'm sorry," I uttered softly, extending my hand. It inched toward my fingers, lightly sniffing them before skittishly jumping back. "I didn't mean to step on you," I added, looking upward to the lit window of our flat.

Dane was home. As soon as I walked through the door, he would want to talk about what I'd tried all day to forget. I stepped back, taking one last look at the complex before turning around and heading toward the riverbank.

Comforted by the dark, abysmal waters, I walked the edge of the Seine under the dim streetlamps, huddled in my coat. Only last winter, I'd been at Camp Wadsworth complaining about the cold with the rest of them. Now, there were only ghosts to talk to.

I stepped up on the embankment, feeling around for the Colt in my pocket.

"Don't do it."

I froze, unloading the last of the bullets into my palm.

"It's not worth dying for, whatever it is."

The wind blew the top of my hair as I glanced over my shoulder toward the Eastern accent. A young woman studied me, pointing to the gun. "Posez le pistolet."

"I heard you the first time."

The silver of her cat-like eyes were accentuated by her black babushka. "I thought so. I overheard you talking to yourself."

I looked down at the waves, softly lapping below, and loosening my grip on the pistol, I allowed it to fall into the water. "I was getting rid of it," I said, dropping the bullets in one-by-one. "A pacifist has no need for a gun."

"It didn't cost me anything to ask."

I nodded, stepping down. "Do you spend all your nights saving lost souls on the rue?"

She turned to the whipping wind and held out her hand, grabbing the attention of the oncoming headlights. "There's my car," she said. "Have a good night."

I watched as she hurried to the curb, walking around back to the other side of the taxi. As many times as I'd walked the Seine at night, I'd never seen her around before, and I might never see her again.

"Miss—" I opened the passenger door opposite her. "I've been waiting for a car, too, do you mind?"

She shook her head, and I climbed in the back seat, trying to keep a respectable distance.

"Where to?" asked the driver.

"Montmartre," she replied.

I raised an eyebrow at her, sporting my most innocent smile. "What do you know? I'm meeting a friend in Montmartre tonight."

Despite my best effort to engage the mysterious woman on the drive, she kept mostly to herself, seemingly content to stare ahead with her hands in her lap. A polite nod was all I got when we parted ways, and the cab left, stranding me in Montmartre with nothing to do. Posted up on the nearest building, I pulled out my pack of cigarettes, watching as she crossed the lively street, scattered with Paris' finest and sloppiest nightlife. I shielded the flame from the wind, lighting one just in time to see her walk into a small corner establishment with a red lantern hanging out front: *Le Royal.*

Puffing on my cigarette, I sauntered across the rue to get a better look—passing an inebriated patron on his way out the door. I took a long drag and looked up at the sign. I'd been to a brothel once with some of the guys from the 108th when we'd first arrived in France, but that had been my experience at length. I hadn't touched any of the girls. But tonight, I was itching with curiosity.

Flicking my cigarette to the ground, I walked through the doors of *Le Royal* to look for the girl with the cat eyes.

I strolled through the main foyer to the back of the house, past a few ladies staggered on the staircase with crowns of peacock feathers and golden chains adorning their heads. The warm, fragrant haze of opium lingered in the air, as thick as the muffled sounds of pleasure it carried. I scanned the tangle of half-naked men and women who lay across the embroidered silk pillows with pipes, but the one I sought was nowhere to be found.

Instead, I caught the eye of a topless woman with waved, golden locks. "Something I can help you with, honey?" she asked, tugging on her gold necklace.

"I don't know," I replied, kneeling before her. "Can you?"

Her lips curled into a devilish grin. *"Sacrebleu,* look at those eyes," she gushed. "Sit with us."

The gentleman next to her readjusted himself, shifting the girl on his lap to make room for me on the sofa. His escort watched me with eyes as dark as the new moon as I sat down next to them. "Bonjour," she said to me.

I nodded hello, watching his greedy fingers caress her bronze shoulder.

The blonde scooted closer and grabbed onto my arm. "Are you looking for a good time tonight?"

"I'm looking for someone specific." I leaned in so she could hear me above the noisy parlor. "I saw her walk in."

"Describe her for me."

"Well, she's…"

Distracted by a nudge to the arm, I turned to see the man next to me offering the long pipe. Hesitantly, I accepted.

"Le Brune Fee?" asked the blonde.

I held the pipe in my hands, examining its gold-leaf pattern and jade mouthpiece. "How do you do it?"

"Like this," she whispered, gently pulling me onto her. "Lie back."

Resting my head on her bare chest, I settled in. "Now," she instructed, guiding the mouthpiece to my lips, "breathe as deeply as you can."

I closed my eyes and inhaled, feeling her fingers creep across my chest. When I could take in no more, I handed the pipe off to her and began to cough. "She's about five foot two, light eyes, Eastern accent," I explained. "I think it's Russian."

"You must mean *Tatiana*," she replied, blowing smoke. "Our Romanov princess."

I coughed again. "A princess?"

"We're all royal here," she teased, motioning to her gold laurel wreath. "I'm Helen, can't you tell?"

"Ahh." I smirked, humored. "Helen of Sparta or Troy?"

"Whichever you want."

Light as a feather, her words seemed to float over me as I gripped the bottom of the sofa, feeling myself sink further into her. I gazed ahead at the painting of a peacock that hung in the corner of the room, feeling my eyelids become heavy, and my mouth become dry.

Picking something off my cheek, Helen brought her finger into my focus. "Make a wish," she whispered.

I squinted at the eyelash that sat on the tip.

"What do you desire most?"

I inhaled, shifting my thoughts to the radiant girl I'd spent the day with. Able to envision her vividly looking back at me, I blew the eyelash.

In front of me, the man laid his head back in a deep slumber. I grinned at his companion, who looked drowsily over his shoulder at me. She reached for my hand—*my hand*—I'd forgotten about it, sitting there on my knee. The minutes passed without authority as she laced her slender fingers in mine, as if time were bending, and I'd fallen comfortably between the creases.

I closed my eyes and drifted downstream amid a sweet midsummer's dream, to a realm I'd thought accessible only through the ink and quill of Shakespeare himself.

"Who's the boy?"

I imagined the voice belonging to a serene face, her hair of ebony beauty, wading through lily pads to meet me in periwinkle velvet. Alongside her was another—with auburn curls and rosy cheeks.

"He's here for Vanina."

"He's beautiful."

The first faery girl nuzzled my cheek. I turned and opened my mouth, meeting her halfway for a kiss.

The other stood by, grabbing onto my hand. *"Couldn't we share him?"* she asked.

"No, I said he's here for Vanina."

Standing offshore, in a dress with puffed sleeves and red sash in front, a crown of orange blossoms sitting atop her bobbed chestnut hair, was a third faery girl. I squinted in inscrutable recognition at her green eyes, framed by sun-kissed freckles, and how they mirrored mine.

"What's your name?" she asked.

"Holden."

The faery Queen stepped forward. "Holden," she repeated.

I tried to burn her features into my mind, but she was as slippery and ephemeral as the vague spark of a lost memory.

Reaching for my face, she whispered in my ear, "don't stay too long here."

"Stop trying to change his mind!"

I reached through the ether as she pulled away, grabbing onto her wrist to pull her back to me.

"But he's sweet...and he likes me."

I raised my eyelids to find myself surrounded by a bevy of women with curious, dreamy expressions, deep in observation. I reached my arm back to the pillow behind my head as the ladies gossiped in hushed tones.

"You were right—they're just like sapphire."

"Vanina has all the luck."

The Arabian beauty I'd held hands with—who I'd come to

know later as Cleopatra—sat on the floor next to me. "You like me, don't you?" she asked, setting her chin on my shoulder.

I smirked. "Very much."

"I bet he's a gentle lover," another cooed from above, running her fingers across my cheek. "Aren't you?"

"I found your Tatiana!"

I looked over to see Helen walking toward us, and behind her, a Tsarina in slinky black lingerie—her cool, beige wave finally visible.

"The girls are all gathered around him like he's a stray kitten," Helen snickered over her shoulder.

"He took a little ride with the dragon," added one of them, hanging her arm over the back of the couch. "We were just waiting for him to wake up is all."

The girl from the river looked down on me, her marvelous gray eyes alight with suspicion. I smiled at her, showcasing my pearly whites.

"Visiting a friend, hm?"

Feeling like I might burst into laughter, I turned away as my fingers danced along Cleopatra's shoulder. "If you don't want him, give him to me," she whined.

I lifted myself off the sofa, feeling the sudden weight of my body. "Thank you for the kiss but I have to go now," I uttered, leaning over and planting one of my own on the downturned pout of my admirer. I smiled and nodded to the rest of the girls, reaching for the extended hand of my Russian princess.

"Take good care of him!" one of them called after us.

My escort held her arm around my waist to steady me as we headed upstairs, past a few rooms rotating with guests. "I don't take well to being followed," she said. "What do you want?"

"Sorry," I replied, nauseous. "I didn't catch your name."

"Tatiana."

With my arm around her shoulder, she shut the door behind us. Dizzily, I looked around the plush room, draped in blue velvet and low light. Even the radiator was painted with evocative scenes. Quick to get started, she ran her hands through my hair and down my chest.

"Do you mind if I lie down?" I asked.

She let go of me and walked over to the bed, taking a seat on its edge. "You shouldn't have touched the pipe," she said. "I didn't take you for the type."

"And I didn't take you for a working girl," I replied, flicking the crystal icicle of the nearest lamp before wandering over and collapsing on the bed next to her. "It's a little strange to be masquerading as the dead, don't you think?"

Her eyes dropped to the floor, then back to me on the bed. "All right," she said, kneeling down. "Lie back, and I'll make this quick for both of us."

I lifted my head to look at her, meeting her gaze as she hovered over my knees.

"I'm assuming you don't want to do any work," she added. "Just lie back, and I'll take care of you. You'll forget about it soon."

I looked up, focusing on the teal ceiling and twinkling crystal chandelier above my head. Sinking back into the high, I closed my eyes, feeling her unlatch my belt and tug on my pants.

"Wait—" I lifted my head again.

She sighed. "I really don't want this to take any longer than it needs to."

"I don't want you to."

"What?"

"I can tell you don't want to," I added. "I don't want to force you."

She lifted her chin, eyeing me dubiously. "You're paying me," she countered. "It feels the best when you're chasing the dragon. At least, that's what they say."

I laughed, stretching my arms behind my head. "Or…maybe I'm wrong. Maybe you *do* want to."

That got her on her feet.

"It's not that I doubt your ability," I added, reaching to buckle my belt. "I'm just not in the mood."

She tilted her head, looking at me as if I had two. "You do know where you are, right?"

"I didn't come here for a good time."

"Then why?" she pressed. "Why go through the trouble of following me in?"

"You thought you were talking me off the ledge earlier," I replied, glancing up at her. "Why wouldn't I want to know your name?"

She took a seat next to me, scanning me over. "How old are you, anyhow?" she asked.

"Twenty-four."

"You're just a boy."

"*Hey*," I cautioned playfully. "Trust me. You wouldn't be saying that if we'd made it any further."

"Are you always so brash?" She pursed her lips in a conflicted smile. "I have a hard time believing you want nothing from me."

"Conversation isn't nothing. I'll pay you the same."

Seeming satisfied, she laid down next to me, and I groaned, turning my cheek to face her. "I think I'm going to be sick."

"Here," she said, rolling me onto my side. Wrapping her arms around me, she laid her cheek against my shoulder blade.

"Can I tell you a secret?" I whispered, closing my eyes. "You can't judge me."

"That's what the money is for."

"I kissed a faery earlier."

"*Vile*. That's what we call them."

"In Russia?"

"Judging from your accent, you're a foreigner, too."

"We're all foreigners." I sighed, feeling her breathing synchronize with mine. "I'm from the States."

"You're a soldier."

"I was."

"Do you still feel sick?" she asked.

"Not as long as I keep my eyes closed." Drowsily, I reached for her hand. "My name is Holden, by the way," I added. "It's nice to meet you."

"*Vanina,*" she said. "My name is Vanina."

LADY
PARIS, DECEMBER 14, 1918

FEELING a hand brush through my hair, I grinned, opening my eyes just enough to be blinded by the sun coming through the window.

"Time to wake up."

I squinted upward to see Jeanne sitting cross legged, staring at me. I tried to regain the fuzzy timeline of the night, but it had faded with the opium. "I was having the most wonderful dream," I mumbled, forcing myself to sit up alongside her.

"I could tell."

"I'm sorry if I kept you up," I said, reaching for my pack of cigarettes on the bedside table.

"And I'm sorry I'm not who you were hoping to wake up next to this morning." Her eyes circled my face—dark and probing. I braced myself. "Though, I'll admit," she added, watching me strike a match, "it was nice to be held all night."

I rubbed my eyes. "What are you talking about?"

"You really don't remember, do you?"

Fuck. Suddenly petrified by the long list of things I could've said under the influence, I felt my anxiety spike.

Jeanne raised a villainous eyebrow. "Care to tell me who Camille is?"

"Who?"

"You couldn't *stop* saying her name last night. Camille, Camille…" she cooed, flopping back on the bed in her silken nighty. "She must really be something if you're thinking about her while I'm—"

"Why do you care, Jeanne? What I do and whom I think about?" I leaned over the edge of the bed, searching the floor for my clothes. "It's really none of your business," I added, flicking into the ashtray. "I don't ask about who you're seeing."

"Because—"

I turned to her, expectant.

"Maybe I don't want to share you."

I took a shallow breath, trying to suppress the cough I felt coming on. "What are you saying?" I stammered.

"Are you *serious*, Holden?" She gawked at me, flummoxed by the notion that I could be so stupid. "Do I really need to say it? The things I've done for you, in public, for God's sake."

"Do you have to word it like that? You were the one who offered!"

"Because *I love you.*"

I snubbed the cigarette and flipped the blanket over, grabbing my pants. "Jeanne, you hardly know me," I said, struggling to get them on. "What happened to free love?"

"Go fall in love," she said, approaching me. "Then come back and tell me how free you are."

"I'd save myself the trouble."

"Mon beau diable. Ange déchu." She grazed her fingers across my cheekbone pensively, then lifted my chin to look at her. "You're not as cynical as you want people to believe."

I frowned.

"You don't love her, do you?" she asked. "Say you don't."

"I don't."

She wrapped her arms around my neck and kissed me, her lips tinged with desperation. I turned my cheek, but refusing to take the hint, she ran her fingers down the length of my shirt buttons, biting onto my shoulder gently.

"Jeanne," I pleaded. "Stop."

"Oh, you want to be a gentleman, now?" she taunted, shoving me away. "Just admit it—you'll never love anyone as much as yourself."

"If that's what you really think," I countered sharply, rebuttoning my shirt, "then you don't know the first thing about me."

Her eyes burned with resentment. "You *are* smitten with her, though, aren't you?" she asked. "Whoever the hell she is."

"We only just met."

"But she's a good listener, right? Do you send her roses and tell her all the things that keep you up at night?"

Ignoring her, I swiped my coat from the floor and swiftly pulled it over, brushing my hair back. "I won't be back," I muttered, walking back to the nightstand to grab my cigarettes.

"I'll believe it when I see it."

"I promise I won't," I said, halting at the door to look at her.

"Then what are you waiting for!" She swiped her hand across her vanity's top, sending everything to the floor. *"Leave!"*

The fragile perfume bottles shattered, spilling their contents across the hardwood, filling the room with a fragrant silence. Jeanne sighed, and looking like she might cry, dropped to her knees. I walked over, kneeling beside her.

"Are you going to see her again?" she asked quietly. "This Camille?"

"Yes," I admitted, carefully collecting the stray shards of glass.

"When you tire of her...feel free to break your promise." Her eyes met mine with a long, drawn-out pause. "She should know that a face like that will never belong to one woman alone."

The kitten peeped out of the alley when I returned that morning, as if it were waiting for me to get back. "Hey, moon eyes," I greeted, crouching to its level. To my surprise, my furry pal approached me, close enough for us to finally get a good look at one another. It couldn't have been more than six weeks old. "You're just using me for food," I remarked, retracting my hand. "I know—we're all doing the best with what we have, aren't we?"

When I walked through the apartment door, Dane was sitting at the table with his arms crossed and the welcome was much less friendly. "Thanks for letting me know you'd be out all night," he uttered.

"I'm always out all night."

"Yesterday was different. After what happened—"

"I was overstimulated." I shut the door behind me. "That's all."

He exhaled in defeat, knowing better than anyone that the more he pushed, the further I'd retreat. "If you won't talk to me about it, at least write about it," he said finally.

Write? I looked at him with a soured expression. "I haven't written anything but letters since before the war."

"I'm sure it would come back to you if you tried. Your worst experience can become your greatest muse."

He was probably right. Like some sort of predetermined contract, I was always going to be a writer, and I'd known it early on. But if I was born with a pen in my hand, it was always Dane who'd encouraged me to put it to paper.

"I don't even have a typewriter anymore," I added, adjusting my coat awkwardly.

"Sure, you do," he said, pulling a few bills from his pocket and nudging me to take them. "For my—" He halted mid-sentence, interrupted by a high-pitched *mew*.

I grinned guiltily, trying to stifle my laughter.

"—for my coat," he finished. "You didn't."

"It's freezing out," I argued, allowing the kitten to climb up the inside of my coat and peek her head over the neckline. "This is Lady."

"Lady?"

I smiled, feeling the warm fur brush across the bottom of my jaw. "Lady MacBeth."

IN THE SUMMER
VIRGINIA, JUNE 17, 1907

I WIPED sweat from my brow with the back of my wrist, sleepy from the heat of a June afternoon. The swooshing branches of the willow tree blew in the breeze, providing a shady oasis from the sun, and the tempting promise of a summer nap. An open-paged book lay across my lap. I'd already read it front to back twice in the three weeks since I'd borrowed it. Setting my pencil down in the grass, I leaned the back of my head against the bark as the feeling of cool air drifted across my forehead, and my eyelids grew heavier.

ARF! ARF!

I jolted awake.

"Shelby!" Tossing the book aside, I extended my arms wide for the panting black dog bolting my direction. "What are you doing, old man?" I asked, running my hands over his fluffy ears. "I'm surprised you can see out of those eyes."

"Who are you calling old man?"

From my seat beneath the foliage dome, I could see the shined shoes and hemmed pants of my grandad hobbling behind with his cane. "It takes one to know one," he added, pulling back the curtain of willow branches.

Staring down on me in his hunched six-foot-two stature, I met his playful blue eyes with a smirk as I rustled Shelby's thick coat.

"Well, aren't you happy to see me? Come here, my boy!"

I lunged from my seat in the grass and clung onto him, squishing my cheek against his chest. His paisley vest was stained with the smell of pipe tobacco and Irish whiskey.

"You've grown at least an inch since I've seen you last," he remarked.

I beamed up at the familiar, worn face and white stubble. "Last week?"

"Amazing what a few days will do." He lifted his top hat, wiping his brow. "What are you doing out here, hm?"

I sauntered over to the book, swiping it from its place in the grass and handing it off to him. "Don't tell Dane," I pleaded. "He hates when I mark up his books."

He nodded slowly, opening to the center. "Where is that brother of yours, anyway? Holed up with his painting?"

"As usual," I sneered, pushing the hair from my forehead. "I'm going to ask him if I can keep it for my birthday."

"It's your birthday...?"

"Good one, old timer," I replied.

"Old timer — do you kiss your mother with that mouth?"

I grinned.

"Now," he began, reaching deep into his pocket. "For your gift." Bending to my level, he held a coin between his thumb and pointer finger but withdrew when I tried to grab it too fast. "This is a special one," he said sternly. "Some might say, my *most* special. It's no mere piece of eight or token of silver."

Assuming a more serious demeanor, I met his piercing eyes, and he nodded, signaling that I could take it.

"Good boy."

I rotated the coin so that I could read it. *"Victoria Dei Gratia."*

"Victoria by the Grace of God. It's a copper penny from Ireland."

"I don't get it," I said. "What's the big deal about a copper penny?"

"Read the date, lad."

"1843."

"And do you know what happened in 1843?"

I shook my head.

"That's the year your grandmother was born," he replied.

"Grandma Joy? But I never met her—why don't you give it to Dane?"

"Because." He clapped my shoulder. "I'm supposed to give it to you."

"Uh..."

"Don't make those eyes at me, listen here!"

"Yes, sir," I mumbled, trying to conceal my laughter.

"It was the first coin I ever bought. June 16, 1894—two months after she passed." He smiled, cupping my cheek. "Your mother went into labor with you that night. And now," he said, closing my fingers over it, "it's yours to do as you see fit."

I gripped the penny in my hand. "I won't lose it," I assured him.

"I know you won't," he replied, standing erect. "Take me inside, my boy. This *old timer* needs to have a seat." He twirled his cane, glancing over my shoulder as I pocketed my birthday gift. "Come on, Mr. Shelby. Surely, you're not made for this weather."

Shelby perked his ears and tilted his head, but he seemed in no rush to move from his shady spot in the grass.

"Let's go!" he called.

The dog only stared blindly ahead, until I intervened with a whistle, which summoned him to attention.

"Oh," said Grandad, side-eying me. "I see how it is."

I shrugged as we walked past the old moss-covered stone well with Shelby trailing behind.

"The book you're reading," he began, resting his arm around my shoulder. "The fellow who wrote it—this Whitman...he's quite popular, no?"

"Only one of the greats, Grandaddy."

"What if I told you I met him?"

I broke my neck to look at him. "I'd say you're telling tall tales!"

"I assure you I'm not…" Grandad chuckled to himself, seemingly amused by how starstruck I was. "That's right—when I was laid up for my leg. It was in a manor house across the river."

"Chatham?"

"Good boy. Good memory."

"I remember the story about the Catalpa trees—" I caught my tongue. He didn't need me to regurgitate the story he'd told us last Christmas Eve after one-too-many drinks—he'd been there. He'd *seen* the dismembered limbs piled high against the Catalpa trees.

"Your author had a brother in the 51st New York. He was just a few beds down from me for a time—George, I think was his name."

"And Whitman?" I asked eagerly. "What was he like?"

"Interesting fellow…always writing letters for the soldiers." He halted abruptly, his eyes brightening at the sight of something up ahead.

I craned my neck and looked out, following the trunks of the pine trees to the sky. There, sitting delicately on a branch, I caught a glimpse at what had enchanted him—an Eastern Bluebird, nestled within its thistles. "Grandaddy?"

He turned to me with a jovial smile, as if he'd just remembered that I was standing next to him.

"What were you saying?" I asked.

He cleared his throat and stepped forward with his cane, resuming our walk to the door. "The past is a dreary place, Holden," he said, squeezing my shoulder. "One shouldn't wish to stay there too long."

The house was still, with only the ticking of the grandfather clock to greet us in the foyer.

"Holden? Is that you?" Ma called from the kitchen.

"Yes," I shouted back, closing the door behind Shelby. "Me and only me…" I grinned at Granddad, thinking I was slick.

"Don't let the heat in, it's hotter than Hades out." Brushing her hands against her apron, she peeked around the corner. "Jack! We weren't expecting you until this evening!"

"I was just having a moment with the *old man,* here," he replied, pointing to me with his cane.

Ma hurried over. "Well, come inside!"

Marcie, emerging from the hallway to see the commotion, eyed me mischievously. "What's that?" she asked, pointing to the copy of *Leaves of Grass* in my hand. "Are you writing another *love letter*?"

"No," I scolded, shoving the book into my pocket. "I was reading."

Marcie was quick to play innocent as our mother turned her attention away from Granddad and to us, lifting my chin to wipe a smudge from my cheek.

"*Thirteen,*" she marveled. "You're getting handsomer every year."

"Ma…" I groaned.

"Wash up now," she directed. "Both of you—your father will be home soon. Are you thirsty, Jack?"

Grandad opened his suit coat, revealing the flask seated inside. "A man never shows up for an occasion empty handed."

Ma raised her eyebrow. "How about something more refreshing? I've got lemonade."

"Twist my arm, Madora. Lemonade would be wonderful." He looked behind him to the cloudy-eyed mass of fluff who'd plopped onto the cool wood floors. "Mr. Shelby," he said. "I trust you'll behave yourself."

Marcie and I watched as the two of them walked down the wallpapered hall and into the kitchen until they were both out of sight, leaving only the sound of the dog's panting keeping time with the clock.

Marcie turned to me with an impish giggle. "Dear Dorthia,"

she recited from memory. "My name is Holden, and I live down the street and I—"

"*I'm not writing a love letter!*" I hissed.

"—I live down the street and I think you're very pretty."

"Goddammit, Marcie, I'm warning you."

Her jaw dropped to the floor.

"Go ahead," I added, rolling my eyes. "Tell Ma I took the Lord's name in vain—I'll tell her you read my journal. My private journal."

She smiled. "You mean...the one full of *love letters?*"

We locked eyes momentarily—hers full of fear and mine, vengeance. I lunged for her, reaching for her underarms. Boy, did she holler.

"Hooooolden stop!!!"

"Go on," I taunted, "what were you saying?"

"Let me go!" she yelled, smacking my arm. "I'm sorry!"

"No you aren't!"

"I really am," she pleaded. Roaring with laughter, she lay on her back, red-faced. "I swear!!"

"You swear?"

"Yes!!" she screeched.

"To whom?" I demanded.

"To God!"

I loosened my grip, allowing her to slip away and run for safety. "Now we're even," I called after her.

She stuck her tongue out in retaliation, holding onto the hall corner. "Well, I know what you're getting for your birthday, and—I'm not telling you!"

"Oh yeah?"

She darted into the kitchen, shouting for our mother and leaving me victorious. I fumbled in my pocket for the copper penny and looked to the quiet upstairs, able to imagine Dane seated by our window with his easel. Rounding the stairway post, I patted Shelby once more before trudging up the stairs, out of breath.

"Are you just going to stand there?"

I pushed our bedroom door open with a sigh. "How'd you know it was me?" I asked, plopping myself on my bed stomach first.

"Intuition."

"I didn't want you to stop," I admitted, admiring the watercolor on his easel. "I like watching."

Dane set his paintbrush down and shrugged as he turned to face me, looking so much older than sixteen. "Then you'll have to be much sneakier."

"Well—look here," I said, tossing the coin in the air and catching it. "Grandaddy gave it to me."

"Looks like a penny."

"It is," I replied, holding it to the window light. "But it's special."

"Give it here."

I reached over, pressing it into his palm.

"1843," he read. "That's when Grandma Joy was born."

"How'd you know that?"

His eyes darted up to me. "I have a knack for remembering birthdays."

"Speaking of, I was wondering…" I squirmed on the bed, pulling *Leaves of Grass* from my trouser pocket. "Do you think I could have this one?"

"Did you mark it up?"

I smiled guiltily, opening the worn cover and passing it off to him. "Pretty bad."

"O Captain, My Captain," he read, scanning the comments I'd written in the margins.

"What?" I asked after a time.

"If I didn't know any better, I'd never believe these notes were written by a twelve-year-old."

"*Thirteen*," I corrected.

"Stop trying to grow up so fast." He tossed the book back to me on the bed. "You're whip smart. You know that?"

"Smart enough for Princeton?"

"We'll see."

I grinned from ear to ear. "You know I'm going to be a great writer one day," I boasted. "I'm going to live in Brooklyn, just like Whitman. And I'm going to write for a paper, and then write a book."

Dane smiled, closing one eye to further inspect the penny. "And I'm going to paint."

"And you're going to paint." I fanned the copy of *Leaves of Grass*, suddenly remembering what Grandad had told me. "God —and listen to *this*, Dane…did Grandaddy ever tell you that he met Whitman?"

"What? Where?"

"Here! During the war!"

Dane's expression turned to one of reservation. "Is he already drinking?"

I frowned. "*No*. Well maybe—but it's true!"

"Holden…"

"Walt Whitman had a brother who was hospitalized with Grandaddy across the river. His name was George. Ask him if you don't believe me!"

"I believe you," he assured, turning his profile to the hazy June skies, framed by our bedroom window. "I know better than to ask him about that stuff. He doesn't like to talk about it."

"I know," I muttered. "So…can I?"

"Can you what?"

I held up *Leaves of Grass*. "Keep it. Since it's my birthday, and I ruined it anyway."

He let out a quick laugh. "That's all you want?"

"I like it a lot."

He leaned back in his chair, lacing his fingers behind his head. "Okay, I'll take your real present back then."

"You got me something for my birthday?"

"Materialistic now, are we?" he poked.

"Can I have it?"

"Well, I was going to wait until dinner to give it to you, but... I'll tell you what." He glanced toward his closet door before stationing himself upright, revealing my penny, still in his palm. "We'll flip your coin—if you win, I'll give it to you now."

"Deal."

"You pick first. Heads or tails?"

"Tails," I replied. "Always tails."

"Ah, ah..." He pulled back as I reached for it. *"I'm flipping it."*

I didn't argue.

"Let's see how special your penny really is," he teased, setting the coin on his thumb and flipping it into the air.

I bit my nail as he slapped it on the back of his hand, then grinned up at him slyly. "Tails."

"A deal is a deal," he said, handing it back to me.

Intrigued, I watched as he walked over to his closet door and opened it, pulling a box from the top shelf.

"I figured that—if you're going to become a great writer, you're going to need one of these."

"Jesus Christ," I stuttered, staring in disbelief at the Underwood 5 typewriter box he sat before me on the bed.

"It's yours." He chuckled. "You can open it, you know."

"But..."

"It's already paid for."

"But how'd you get the money?"

He motioned to his easel by the window. "You said it yourself —I'm getting pretty good."

"You sold something to buy me this?"

"I figure you can repay me by letting me illustrate your stories when you're rich and famous and I'm a starving artist in New York."

Taking a seat next to me on the bed, he pushed the box closer to me, persuading me to open it. "Consider me your benefactor."

A Tempting Coincidence
Paris, December 24, 1918

Sprawled back on the blue Persian rug, I stretched one arm over my head, reaching for her.

"No tickling," Camille whined, writhing away from my fingers that brushed her shoulder. "I thought we called a truce."

I smiled to myself, recalling the frenetic play that had landed us here, temple to temple across the floor of her family's sitting room, covered in the dusty remnants of an all-out flour war. Hand-painted Greek revival clouds hung above our heads on the ceiling, framing a romantic depiction of Venus disarming Mars.

"What are you going to do while I'm gone?" she asked, grabbing my hand.

I bumped her temple with mine, gazing up at the cupids with angel wings. "Sit around and miss you."

She cackled. "Oh—*stop!*"

I rolled onto my stomach, adjusting myself above her, cheeks sore from laughter. "I should be asking you the same question," I countered. "What are *you* going to do when you have no one to throw flour at?"

"I'll simply have to find another baking partner," she replied. "Maybe a nice Londoner."

My eyes shot up to the vase of red roses sitting gracefully on the oak buffet—how nice they looked next to the porcelain clock, whose hand was ticking away too fast. "And will he bring you a dozen roses, too?" I asked.

Her upside-down smile beamed up at me. "I should certainly hope so."

"I don't," I said lowly, wiping flour from the side of her nose with my thumb.

"You sound worried," she teased. "Do you take me as someone who's easily bored?"

"Basically, I'm just dumb. I start to like someone, and I get these ideas in my head." I paused, shrugging coolly. "I'd hate for you to find an English chap to bake scones with."

"Are you sure you can't come along?"

"Dane and I haven't spent a Christmas together in years," I replied, pressing my forehead to hers. "I can't leave him high and dry the first time we get the chance." I lifted my head, smirking at her weakly. "Besides, I just bought a new typewriter. This gives me a chance to get acquainted."

"Admit it. I'm merely distracting you from your life's work."

"A welcome distraction." I dropped my lashes, pecking the top of her cheekbone. "Should we check on the dough?"

"Oh—we've got another thirty minutes at least before it's finished rising."

"So then…" I touched both of her shoulders, leveraging myself further over her with a suggestive smile. "What should we do in the meantime?"

"It seems I should be asking you."

"Well, we could…"

She widened her eyes in a playful manner, coaxing me to go on.

"It's Christmas Eve."

"I suppose you find Christmas particularly romantic?"

"Well…"

"Or perhaps you're asking for your present."

"Don't tease me. There are nicer ways to say no."

She reached up, taking my face in both hands. "I'm not saying no."

I raised my brows, looking at her with full attention.

"How would you set the scene?" she asked, pulling me to her. "Show me."

"Like this," I whispered, covering her face in delicate kisses. "Just...like this."

Camille sat upright, unbuttoning my vest in a haste. I caressed the back of her neck, allowing her to drag me back down to the floor.

"Did you hear that?" she whispered, tilting her head toward the foyer.

"No," I murmured, cupping her cheek and turning it back to face me. "Come here."

"It sounded like a car door."

"It's the street."

"It sounded like it was right outside."

Hellbent on preserving our moment of eros, I paid her no mind—until the crisp sound of someone's knuckles on the door broke through to my rational mind. I looked down at her, mirroring her agape expression.

"*See?*"

"Swell way to meet your family," I whispered sharply.

The knock clamored across the wood a second time, and slowly, with my eyes glued to the front door, I lifted myself off of her.

"Who on earth?" She darted to the window and ripped the curtain to its side, nearly tripping over her own two feet. "It's Marge!"

"Who?" I asked, trying to beat out the flour we'd tracked onto the antique velvet sofa with my vest. What a waste of perfectly good flour.

"*Marge*—my cousin," Camille huffed. "She wasn't supposed to be here until evening." Running her fingers across her chin, still flushed from my stubble, she groaned. "I have to let her in!"

"All right."

"Act normal," she ordered, disappearing around the corner.

Hands in my pockets, I scanned the vacant, opulent sitting room. It was filled with seventeenth century furniture and irreplaceable items worth ten times my military pension. Feeling the inferiority start to seep in, I turned my attention back to the vase of roses, waiting patiently in place as I heard the footsteps and conversation draw closer.

"And this is Holden," said Camille, popping around the corner.

"*The* Holden?"

I pursed my lips together in a futile attempt to smother my grin.

Marge—a tiny thing, much shorter than Camille, with auburn hair and an impassive but pretty face—trailed behind her. "My, you two have really made a mess of things," she noted.

Fix your hair, Camille mouthed.

Marge tilted her head, inspecting me as I did what I was told. "It really is a mess in here," she said. "What did you bake? Are we bringing it to Christmas?" She eyed me. "Is *he* coming…?"

"No," I interjected. "I'm spending Christmas with my brother."

She turned to Camille. "He has a brother?"

"He does. We were waiting for the dough to rise when you knocked," Camille explained, fidgeting with her fingers. "You know how that is."

"Speaking of which—it should be ready now," I said, walking over to join the girls. "Should we see?"

"Yes! Join us, won't you Marge?"

"Oh, I don't know."

"I insist." I offered my arm, watching her dubious frown vanish before my eyes.

Seemingly won over, she accepted.

"You know, Marge," I began as we strolled toward the kitchen, "about my brother. I was thinking, maybe after the holiday, the four of us could get together."

Camille gripped the back of my shoulders, following us out. "Wouldn't that be fun!"

I leaned on the back of the chair with a cigarette in my mouth, admiring the glossy shine and nouveau lettering that stretched across the top of my new Royal typewriter. Lady blinked at me with sleepy eyes, tapping her tail on the desk next to it.

"You can't rush perfection." I cleared my throat, flicking my ash onto the dish next to her. "And don't forget," I added, scratching under her chin. "I found you in a dumpster. You have no room to judge me."

Before she could counter me with another of her slow blinks, Dane walked through the front door looking like one of Dickens' Christmas ghosts, tree in tow. "Hey," he said, nodding to me. "How's it going?"

"Just settling in," I replied, distancing myself from the typewriter. "It's been a long time."

He closed the door behind him, shivering from the draft he'd let in. "It wasn't as long ago as it feels, I'm sure."

I sighed, crossing my arms over my nervous heart. "Lifetimes."

"What the hell is all over you?"

"Trying out a new occupation," I joked, brushing the flour off my vest. "I just got back from Camille's an hour ago."

"I thought she was going to London for Christmas?"

"Oh, she is—she just left," I replied, strutting into the kitchen. Lady followed, jumping up on the table as I opened the icebox and grabbed the milk, pouring some into her saucer. "She was supposed to leave yesterday with her parents, but she told them she could catch a ride with her cousin and to go on ahead without her." I popped around the corner with a cheeky grin. "She wanted to see me one more time."

"Well, while you were doing God knows what on her sofa, I was out finding us a tree," he said, motioning to the potted table tree that he held in his arms like a baby.

"You mean finding us a shrub," I corrected. *"Doing God knows what on her sofa,"* I mimicked, grabbing the plate of pastries on my way out. "What do you take me for, some kind of deviant?"

Lady's tail twitched with curiosity as he set the tree down on the windowsill, but she didn't budge.

"Her cousin was there anyway," I added, biting into one of the pastries.

"Those look decadent."

"At least two weeks' worth of sugar. Here, have one." I extended the plate to him. "They're blueberry."

He obliged, biting into one reluctantly. "So why didn't you go, then?" he asked.

"Go where?"

"Why didn't you go to London with her?"

"What—and leave you here alone?" I motioned to the flakey pastry in his hand, and the satisfied look on his face. "They're good, aren't they?"

"Something tells me Camille did most of the work," he said, going in for a second bite. "Really, it's the *butter.*"

I set the plate down. "She said I was a natural."

"We can bring them along tonight."

"We're still going?" I asked, mouth full.

He gave me a look as if I should know better. "It's a new moon."

"But it's frigid out."

"The colder the air, the crisper the sky." He pulled a bottle of wine from his bag, handing it to me. "This should keep you warm."

"Look at us, living like kings." I studied the bottle's cursive label, written in unreadable French—at least to me. "Looks expensive."

"It was a gift for finishing the commission early."

I smirked, handing it back to him. "How generous."

It was around eleven when we headed out to Bois de Vincennes, away from the city lights that polluted the skyline. A knapsack sat between us in the taxi, its contents filled with holiday cheer—the nice bottle of wine, two considerably shittier bottles of wine, and a little meat and cheese to go along with the pastries. I shivered, tucking my chin into the bundled scarf around my neck.

"Just like old times," teased Dane, turning to me. "Remember?"

"As if I could forget." I smiled faintly. "How do you think the parents would feel if we told them how much of our adolescence was spent sneaking out the bathroom window to stargaze?"

"We're taking that one to the grave," he retorted. "I can't have your mother thinking I endangered her beloved first born."

"Remember when I had to bribe Marcie after she caught us that night?"

"Wait—you bribed her?"

"Of course I did!" I laughed, loosening my scarf. "She gave me an ultimatum—either we take her with us on the roof or I give her one of Granddad's coins. Of course I chose the coin."

"Which one?"

"One of the silver dollars. Between that and giving Jamie that piece of eight before I left, I don't have any of them anymore."

"What about Grandma's penny?"

"Lost it in Ypres."

Dane nodded to himself, rubbing his chin with his hand. "We should've just taken her up," he said. "Her and Jamie both. We should've included them more."

"I guess at the time, I didn't want to share it," I admitted. "But you're right. We should've."

"Lac Daumesnil is fine," said Dane, suddenly clutching the front seat.

The car rolled to a stop, and I reached for the handle, throwing the knapsack over my shoulder. It took a minute for my eyes to adjust as the headlights of the car disappeared down the road.

"You coming?"

Swinging the knapsack around front, I sprinted after Dane under the shadow of the trees.

"Not a bad view for just outside of the city, is it?" he called back to me.

I nodded to myself, noting the lake to our right. "I'd say it's even better than the roof," I replied, fiddling with the cork of the first wine bottle as I lagged behind.

"I think this should do right here," he directed. "Everything should come up just over that horizon."

"If we don't freeze to death first."

From the edge of the glassy lake, we found ourselves caught in a reflective lattice of ancient asterisms—their stars on fire, flickering resistantly against a timeless void.

"Funny," I murmured, studying the sky. "Funny that something so peaceful can be so equally volatile."

"Do you want to know what we're looking at?"

"Of course I do." I took a sip from the bottle, handing it off to my brother. "Pollute my mind with your pagan stories."

"Well," he began, "there's Orion to the south, with Taurus—"

"And Gemini," I added, squinting closely.

"And Gemini."

I laughed to myself.

"What?"

I paused, lying the knapsack on the ground and plopping down next to it as he stood at the edge of the lake, recreating a tableau of our childhood. "I used to tell that story to the guys… but I could never tell it as well as you could." I looked up to see Dane extending the bottle to me. "How does it go, again? I want to make sure I have it right if I ever find myself in another war."

We split the first bottle and moved onto the second, waiting for the stars to rise in the same way we had as kids.

"I'd kill for Ma's brisket right now," I whined, sorting through the contents of the knapsack.

"I'm insulted," Dane teased, launching a pastry corner at my face.

"Easy for you to say. It's been—what, a decade since you've had it?"

"It hasn't been a decade."

"Sorry—" I turned to him with a smile. "*Half* a decade."

"Christmas 1914. You met me at Grand Central and we took a train down together. Remember?"

"My first semester at Princeton."

Dane laughed to himself. "You were so wired the whole way down, and I was exhausted from the trip—I could hardly keep my eyes open."

"You were saving all your energy for dinner table politics," I poked.

"I really thought you were playing devil's advocate that night. I never thought you'd actually join up if the States entered the war."

"For the record, I *was* playing devil's advocate that night." I paused to take a sip of wine. "I wouldn't bother to debate you on it now."

"I have a lot of questions."

I smirked, holding the mouth of the bottle against my lip. "And I'm not nearly drunk enough to answer them."

"You know, you could always go back."

"What do you mean?"

"Schools are letting veterans finish their degrees."

It would've been the perfect opportunity to tell him why I would never set foot back on Princeton soil, but I swallowed the shame, returning it to the pit of my stomach. "I couldn't go back. Not after all of this."

"Fair enough," he replied, brushing the dead grass with the bottom of his palm. "Hard to believe that was our last Christmas Eve together anyway."

"Do you miss it?" I asked. "Home? I always wondered if you did, all the way over here."

I sat the bottle down between us, and he picked it up, trying to gauge how much of it I'd drank. "Of course. I imagine home would feel pretty foreign to me now, though."

"To you and me both." I brought my knees up, wrapping my arms around them. "This feels right. The two of us, across the world—with a fair chance of hypothermia."

He leaned over and ruffled my hair as if I was twelve years old, and I swatted him away. "You have a peculiar way of telling me you love me," he said.

"At least I tell you." I snatched the bottle back from him playfully, glad to finish it off.

"But now that we've opened the floor for that discussion," I began, lying back, "how do you know?"

"How do you know what?"

I gazed upward at the quiet star patterns, feeling the wine take hold. "How do you know if you love someone?"

I could hear him shift to look at me. "What about that girl from New York? Didn't you love her?"

I shrugged, crossing both arms over my chest. "Sometimes I wonder," I whispered, watching my breath freeze in the air above me. "How many lifetimes I've searched for her in the stars. Whoever she is...or was."

"It's in your nature."

I turned my head with a sigh, listening to Dane uncork the third bottle. "What do you mean by that?"

"If anyone were to spend lifetimes pining for their other half, it would be Gemini."

"Maybe so," I said, reaching into my coat pocket for my pack of cigarettes. "Or maybe I just get sentimental when I drink."

"And when you make pastries."

I chuckled to myself, striking a match. "There's something else. Have you ever heard of a place called *Le Royal?*" I asked, coughing on the exhale. "In Montmartre?"

"Don't tell me you're on the pipe now."

"No." I flicked my cigarette ash, then went in for another drag. "There's a girl there I've been going to see."

"Then you're not in love," he replied.

"It's just a passing fancy," I said, sitting up. "Nothing more."

"There's usually a lot going on behind the scenes for those women."

"What's your point?"

"I'm only saying that you have enough of your own problems."

"Thanks, brother." I laughed sharply under my breath, reaching for the bottle. "Better not let me forget."

"That came out wrong."

"That doesn't make it false," I replied, trying to drown the bitterness with another gulp of wine.

"Sorry. I'm too honest when I drink."

"Then tell me—did you kill anyone when you were in Italy?"

Dane grabbed the bottle from my hand. "Once or twice," he admitted, holding it sternly. "Occasionally you'd come across someone that you just couldn't help. It wasn't right to let them suffer."

I stared across the lake with a glazed expression. He wouldn't want to know my number. I'd long lost track. "What does it say about me that I find comfort in the most malefic of the heavenly bodies?" I asked, lifting my eyes to the red planet gleaming angrily on the horizon.

"I'd say the God of War is a good ally to have."

"Of course. Blood, iron and rage."

"People forget that everything Mars stands for, he also stands against," he reminded. "He's the villain and the hero."

"A toast, then." I raised the wine bottle to the sky. "To Mars—may you live long, and may I never die."

"To Mars," Dane repeated, taking a swig of his own.

"Listen…" Drunkenly, I felt around in my pocket for Rick's necklace. "Do you want this? I found it when I was looking through my suitcase."

"What is it?"

"An old religious pendant," I said, dropping the chain into his palm. "Do you want it or not? It's…"

"Saint Stephen." He held his breath, trying his best to make out the carving under the midnight sky. "Are you going to tell me where it came from?"

"It belonged to my first Lieutenant."

"The Lieutenant from the hospital?"

"The other one."

"Rick."

"Yeah. Rick."

We'd been clearing fortifications around St. Quentin when I caught wind of an ammunition depot in one of the entrances we'd uncovered. I was confident that the tunnel had been secured when we entered, but the pair of stowaway brothers had taken us by surprise. Rick had died under *my* command. My carelessness. And he wasn't the only one. There was Mullins—goddammit, poor Mullins—all blown to shreds. Then there was Pitman, who got a bullet between his eyes. There was something to be said for it being quick, though, unlike Thelander. Beckham's death was the only one who hadn't inadvertently been my fault.

"Holden."

"Hm?"

"*I said* you should keep it then," said Dane, handing it back. "You never think about wearing it?"

"You know I don't follow any of that anymore," I replied, pocketing the necklace with a shrug. "I can't tell you how long it's been since I've taken mass."

"For what it's worth, Saint-Étienne-du-Mont is only a five-minute walk from our flat."

I looked at him blankly.

"The Church of Saint Stephen," he repeated in English. "It's the gothic cathedral. You can't miss it."

"A tempting coincidence." I laid back with a sigh, lacing my fingers behind my head. "But it was never in *God's plan* for me to stay a Catholic."

PAST THE GLASS
NEW YORK CITY, AUGUST 1917

"Miss? Miss! Excuse me," I called, hanging onto the edge of the desk. "My friends and I would like to have our portraits taken?"

The curvy brunette clerk slipped the pencil she was holding behind her ear, keeping her eyes on the appointment book. "You and every other guardsman in the city," she remarked, not bothering to look up at me.

I scanned the packed photography studio, glancing over my shoulder to see that Beckham and Spofford had trickled through the glass door behind me.

"Miss…"

"I told you, we're busy—" She lifted her eyes to mine.

I smirked at her. "Hi."

Dropping her shoulders, she reached behind her ear to fiddle with the pencil. "Hi," she murmured back. "Sorry, what I mean to say is that we're a little booked up."

"Is there any way I could convince you to squeeze in three more?"

The clerk looked past me to see Beckham and Spofford standing erect in their stiff, fresh greens—pockets full of bubblegum and candy from the parade.

"See, we don't know when we'll have the time to go to a studio once we're in Spartanburg," I added.

"Well, I..."

I leaned over the desk, tapping the corner with my thumb. "What's your name?"

"Irene."

"Irene." I dropped my voice to a musky whisper. "If there was anything you could do, I'd really appreciate it." When I looked up, she was blushing.

"I could fit you in at 3:15," she squeaked. "Come with me."

We followed Irene to the back of the house, passing hordes of soldiers clutching their rifles with clammy hands as they waited for their turn in front of the lens.

"I guess everyone else had the same idea as us," Beckham noted.

"When do you leave for training?" asked Irene, turning back to me.

"Friday."

"The parade was really something. I watched it from the window," she went on. "I'm only sorry I had to work—I would've liked to see it up close."

"I'm glad you were here."

She reached for the pencil again, bashfully meeting my eye. "Well, here we are," she said, bringing us to the end of the line. "Dora will come get you when it's your turn."

"Sounds great."

"I'd better get back up front."

"Thank you again."

She grinned, biting her lower lip before leaving us be.

Watching her scurry away, I counted to see how long it would take her to look over her shoulder at me. One, two, three—*four.* I smiled, meeting her gaze across the room.

"Unbelievable," Beckham mumbled over my shoulder.

"I'll have her in my bed tonight," I said, turning back to my friends.

"How'd you do that?"

Before I could answer, Rick interjected. "Shouldn't ask advice from the devil, Charlie."

"I feel like I should be more offended than I am." I laughed. "What's the matter with you, Beck? You apple-knockers weren't built for this kind of heat, were you?"

"It's not the heat, it's nerves—for fuck's sake." Beckham wiped his forehead with his handkerchief. "I can't believe I let you fellas talk me into this. I hate having my picture taken!"

I smirked, adjusting the necklace in my collar.

"Keep your comments to yourself, you handsome sonofabitch. You're not the one who has to live with this baby face."

Rick clapped him on the shoulder. "Relax. You'll be glad you did."

"He's right," I added, reaching for a cigarette. "In case you give yourself a heart attack before you make it to France."

Rick chuckled to himself, unwrapping a piece of bubblegum and popping it into his cheek.

Beckham glanced toward the front, then back at us, lowering his voice as if we were discussing tactics. "It doesn't help that the camera man's assistant is so…"

Synchronously, we stepped out of line to get a better view of the young girl at the front, studying the shape of her tan skirt as she guided the next subject to his sitting.

"Distracting," I finished, pinching the unlit cigarette between my lips.

"Dora—that's her name, right? How am I supposed to relax with her around?"

"She looks familiar," I added, removing my cigarette and rolling it in between my fingers.

"Familiar how?" asked Rick.

"*God* don't tell me you know her," Beckham groaned.

"I don—"

"It would ruin the fantasy."

"She just reminds me of someone I dated," I said, returning the cigarette to my mouth and lighting it. "Right before I enlisted."

A FEW MONTHS PRIOR————————

The early March chill still lingered on her clothes as I slipped my hand under her back, pulling her to me with an insatiable appetite.

"Hold your horses," she whispered in my ear.

I looked at her innocently as we lay tangled together on her bed with the cuckoo clock looking down on us.

"Are you in a rush?"

I grinned, dropping my voice. "I can't be long. I have rifle practice later."

"But it's Sunday."

"Wars still rage on Sundays."

She wrinkled her nose.

"I'm only kidding, Bonnie," I said, pecking her cheek. "I'm just trying to be the best I can be."

"I'm proud of you," she said, turning away from me. "I really am."

"But..." I added, sensing there was more.

"It's hard to imagine that a few months ago you had no interest in any of this, that's all," she replied. "I don't understand the intensity behind it."

"Well, some would say" —I pressed her against me, eager to get back to it— "that intensity is just unappreciated passion."

"Holden..."

I wasn't listening. I brushed my nose against her temple and started to kiss her neckline. "No one's home."

"Holden!"

"What?"

Grabbing my arm, she squirmed out from under me. "Is this all you want me for now?"

"I can't believe you'd even ask me that."

"It's all you ever think about," she added, shoving me away. "We don't do any of the things we used to do."

"That's completely untrue."

Her eyes found the bedroom window. "You don't even write to me anymore."

"If you don't like it, all you have to do is say so," I snapped.

"Excuse me for not being crazy about you trying to undo my skirt any chance you get. Ever since that first time, it's all you care about. That and your drills."

I rolled onto my back, staring up at the ceiling. "I don't want to spend another afternoon arguing."

"You haven't slept in days, you're getting into fights—"

"I'm in the best shape I've ever been in," I countered. "I finally feel like I'm a part of something."

"And what about me?"

"Just say what you want to say, Bonnie." I sat upright, pushing my hair out of my face. "It's not fair to let me make up stories in my head."

"I know you're going to New York to enlist." She swallowed hard. "Theo told me." I didn't deny it, not even when I looked over to see her wiping a tear that had fallen with the edge of her sweater. "And I know there's nothing I can say to change your mind. I can see it in your eyes."

"You don't want to wait," I said coldly, rising to my feet. "You forget you're not beholden to me."

She reached for my hand, but I tore it away, snatching my sport coat from the end of her bed. Still, she scooted to the edge, demanding my gaze. "The Holden I remember, I'd wait for him night and day."

"You expect me to believe that, Bonnie? You're telling me you want to get married, but you don't even want to make love."

"If we were married, I'd feel differently."

"Fine." I threw on my coat, checking my hair in her vanity mirror. "If we can go two months without quarreling, we'll get married."

"Holden?"

My eyes found her in the mirror.

"If I were pregnant, would you still be leaving?"

I turned around, loosening my collar. "Are you?"

Bonnie shook her head.

"Then I have to go," I said, turning back to the mirror. Whatever faith she had left in me—in *us*—I watched it dissolve in the reflection behind me.

I hustled down her foyer stairs in such a hurry that I didn't even see someone on the other side of the screen door when I pushed it open.

"Oh—hi Faye," I said, snapping to attention. "Sorry…ah, we didn't think anyone was…"

"I'm home early."

"Right! Sorry." I mirrored the smile of the vibrant younger sister—a tall, bottle blonde with downturned lips.

She narrowed her eyes on me, looking amused from her place behind the screen. "Leaving so soon?"

"I've got to get back to campus."

Faye stepped back as I opened the screen door, meeting her face to face on the other side.

"Could you maybe not mention I was here to your parents?" I rubbed the back of my neck. "I don't want to get Bonnie in any trouble."

"Our secret."

"I appreciate it," I said, nodding to her as I stepped down on the second stair. "I'll see you around, Faye."

"I think it's awfully brave," she said suddenly.

"Hm?"

Faye wrung her hands together, as if she were gathering the confidence to say something. "I know Bonnie doesn't want you to go to France," she admitted. "But for what it's worth, I think you're very brave."

. . .

The flash of the camera pulled me back to the present.

"So, this girl," Rick prodded. "What happened?"

Bonnie found me in bed with her sister and told me she never wanted to see me again. That's what happened.

"You know." I shrugged. "They call it young love for a reason."

"That's a shame."

"Is it?" I asked. "I figure it's easier this way. No one to miss."

"That's ice cold," Rick replied, blowing a bubble. "That poor girl at the desk didn't stand a chance."

"What is that thing you keep fiddling with?" asked Beck.

"Oh—this?" I tucked my chin. "My grandad gave it to me when I was a kid," I replied, pulling out the copper penny. "Thought it might be a good thing to bring along, so I had it made into a necklace."

Rick nodded. "Did he fight in the war?"

"Irish Brigade." I paused to tuck it back into my collar. "He died when I was fifteen."

"Hey Beck." Rick nudged his arm. "Look."

We turned in unison to see for ourselves that Dora, now only ten feet or so away, was stretching her neck, scanning the row of orderly uniforms in our collective direction.

The three of us were grinning like a bunch of idiots when Rick finally murmured through his teeth, "Who do you figure she's looking at?"

I was in the midst of holding up my hand to wave when Beckham shot me a few daggers. "Who do you *think*?"

Feeling a shove to the arm, I bumped into Rick, losing her gaze. "Jesus, what's your problem?"

"Don't do that," he hissed. "She's going to fall in love with you!"

"Relax Beck, I'm just being nice."

"Well *don't*. You've already got your date!"

"Are you going to ask her out, then?"

Beckham scoffed as if I'd suggested something outrageous.

"Of course I'm not!"

"If you're not willing to claim your stake, Beck—well," Rick began. The camera flashed, the line shifted, and the three of us with it. "Then all's fair in love and war, ladies."

"We're here til the end of the week," I argued. "What's stopping you?"

"Well, I don't know—maybe the twenty other soldiers who have probably done the same?"

"That's quite the assumption."

"True. We aren't all born with your confidence."

I laughed sharply, wanting to counter, but the fact that I'd been a chaste schoolboy until my junior year would've seemed inconceivable to my new friends.

"I was studying writing before I enlisted," I said. "If I were as confident as you say, maybe I'd still be doing it."

Beckham's face contorted. "Writing? Really?"

"He came from Princeton," Rick added, turning to him to elaborate. "Hoity-toity Ivy League."

"No shit."

"Keep it down," I hushed.

"Is it a secret?"

"I didn't tell the recruiters." I looked over my shoulder. "The last thing I wanted was an officer's position."

A long silence followed, eventually ruptured by Rick's bubblegum.

"I was going to do accounting for the family business," said Beckham.

"Not a bad gig to have when you get back," I noted.

"Yeah." His knitted brow reflected what he wouldn't dare speak out loud.

If he came back.

"I'm good at math, but I hate it," he added.

"I was never smart enough for anything like that," said Rick, who'd worked the New York City docks since he was thirteen. "Europe's war was the best thing that could've happened to me."

"*She's coming,*" said Beckham.

"This way please." Dora's voice oozed with honey as she stepped up to retrieve Rick.

"Wish me luck," he whispered under his breath before abandoning us in line.

Like all who'd gone before him, he donned his most suave impression as she led him over and positioned him. Dora on the other hand, was inscrutable with her inaccessible smile. Warm but distant.

I remembered thinking the same thing about Bonnie when we first met. I'd been writing a paper on the lawn—Scott bullshitting next to me—when he'd spotted Theo and his girlfriend at the edge of campus. I only had to glance upward for my mind to abandon my English homework in favor of studying the friend she'd brought along with her. I had little awareness of my own looks sophomore year, never mind the effect they could have on girls, and if it weren't for Bonnie speaking to me first, I probably would've been too shy to engage her.

She'd been my first real girlfriend. My first everything. And I never even told her I was sorry.

"*Next!*"

Rick nodded thanks to the camera man and walked to the sideline, giving me a confident nod on the way.

"Follow me, please," said Dora.

"Yes, ma'am," I replied.

I glanced over my shoulder at Beckham, who glared with eyes wide, screaming *don't you dare*.

I winked in return.

"I'm going to have you stand right here," she directed, lightly touching my shoulder so I'd angle left. I looked ahead, past her dazzling smile to the camera. "All set," she added, straightening the sleeve of my tunic.

I grinned at her as she stepped aside, then turned my attention forward.

"On the count of three," stated the invisible camera man.

"One...two..."

I lifted my chin stoically, looking into the lens. Past the glass, and into a future I could not yet see.

"Three."

Dora appeared through the haze of my flash blindness, just like an angel.

"In your professional opinion," I began, "do you think it turned out all right?"

"No doubt," she assured, guiding me away from the background as my eyes adjusted. "Blue eyes always photograph beautifully. I hope you have someone special to give it to."

"Not anymore."

"I'm sorry." She slowed her walk back to the line, and I did the same. "I should learn to mind my business."

"She turned me down."

"Oh—she turned you down? Before you go to France? That's the saddest thing I've ever heard."

"I'm holding faith that maybe she'll change her mind." I dropped my eyes to the floor, assuming the look of a dejected soldier whose fiancée had declined his proposal. "I don't know what else to do. I can't imagine my life without her, if I'm being honest with you. She's all I think about."

"I'm so sorry."

"I kept the ring to wear around my neck," I said, showing her the chain in my collar. "Just in case...you know. I would want to have a piece of her with me."

"Goodness."

Just as I was working my magic, we reached the head of the line where Beckham waited. "Thank God for this one. He's been such a comfort to me," I said, grabbing his shoulder. He turned to me, wide-eyed as a screech owl. "I mean it, Charlie. You're the best friend a guy like me could ask for."

"That's so sweet," Dora swooned.

Satisfied with my handiwork, I started toward Rick, flashing him a triumphant grin.

My Aphrodite
Paris, December 25, 1918

I scanned the farm, searching frantically across the fields and over the heaps of fractured wood. A tinge of smoke remained in the air from the bombardment, as pungent in my memory as the scent of her lavender soap. I was in Vooremezle. The old farmhouse was just as I'd remembered.

"Nat?"

I looked up at the chipped white paint, suddenly hit by a nauseating recollection that I'd done this before.

"Nat!" I called out, louder this time.

"You won't find her here."

I bucked at the familiar voice, carried over my shoulder by an August breeze long gone.

"But I'll find you here," I said, turning around.

Rick stood behind me, alive and well, arms crossed, his slate eyes lit by the afternoon sun.

"I find you but never her," I snapped. I could almost feel the splinters in my knuckles from striking the farmhouse door, and the weight of Rick's hand on my shoulder as I'd knelt over the white cross in the ground. "You told me she was in heaven—that day we came back." My eyes filled to the brim with furious tears. "I hope you see now that none of it is real."

I was awoken by the feeling of sandpaper brushing against the salty, tear-streaked side of my nose. I reached for my face. Lady bumped the top of her head against my palm, and I opened my eyes, finding myself still fully clothed from a deep, wine-induced slumber. I rolled onto my back, letting out a long, aching sigh. She brushed my cheek with her whiskery kitten nose.

"I'm sorry, Rick," I whispered, gazing blankly up at the muted-white ceiling. I pulled his pendant from my pocket and dangled it over my chest with the tinsel of the Christmas shrub glittering nearby. It was impossible not to look at it without being reminded of my own necklace, buried six feet under. I sat up and struck a match, expelling the ghosts of blue hour and illuminating the room in a warm glow. Lady's eyes grew wide as they focused in on the flame I held between my fingers. "I just wanted to see her again," I said, watching the fire dance in their reflection. "If only for a pitiful moment."

I climbed off the mattress, transferring the flame to the candle on the desk. The light poured over the blank loose-leaf pages beside the Royal, inviting me to pick up the pencil next to them. But I grabbed my coat from the back of the chair instead.

I needed some air.

As coincidence—or admittedly, my curiosity—would have it, I found myself passing by the church Dane had mentioned. Casting an impressive silhouette against the dusty pink cloudscape, the Saint-Etienne-du-Mont stood stoically in Renaissance style, with stone-carved columns framing the double doors, and a chiseled portrayal of the stoning of Saint Stephen above. Fiddling with the chain in my pocket, I crossed the empty street for a closer look. I dallied at the foot of the half-moon stairs for what felt like forever before I swallowed my pride and pushed the left door open, revealing an empty sanctuary, whose candles at the front flickered in an eerie quiet. The rays of a promising sunrise leaked through the stained-glass windows, and taking in the scene, I couldn't help but think back to the last time I'd been in a church. From where I stood now, I could see hints of the past in the sunlit dust particles—remembering the charred windows of the once grand St. Martin's Cathedral in Ypres, and the ashes that had floated gently through the air like snowflakes.

I made my way to the altar, inspecting the countless prayers and offerings left for the lost husbands and fathers of Europe. Pulling the tangled chain from my pocket, I laid the pendant to rest alongside them. I peered around, glancing once over my shoulder for good measure. When I was confident that I was alone, I closed my eyes and took a knee.

No less than three minutes later, I begrudgingly lifted my lids, annoyed by the sound of shoes on the tile floor just behind me. I watched as a wrinkly hand laid a coin on the shrine, then drew back into a colorful, draped sleeve of an old Romani woman. "There's something beautiful about an empty church, isn't there?" I asked, half-condescendingly.

"It's not empty. You're here," she replied, her accent thick. "I hope you don't mind me joining you."

"No, of course not." I softened my tone. "You don't often see Roma in the city."

"I was called to come by the same thing that called you."

I frowned.

"You disagree," she added.

"All due respect, your God is no one I'd like to know."

The laugh lines around her mouth curled upward. "And yet, you are kneeling."

I stood up, returning her smile. "Enjoy the empty church."

I was halfway down the sanctuary aisle when I heard her mumble something in her native tongue. I halted, resting my hand on the back of the nearest chair.

"Someone is whispering to you," she called to me. "Can you hear them?"

The doors in front of me creaked open, spilling morning sunlight across the tile. *"Drabardi?"* An adolescent girl hugged the doorway, looking past me with her golden-green eyes.

"Or perhaps the question," said the elderly hermit, finding my side, "is whether or not you want to hear what they have to say."

I turned to her. "You tell me, fortune teller."

She reached for my hands, taking them into her icy palms. I looked to the cathedral columns behind her, then to the rails twirling down the double staircases.

"You live among your dead," she said. "In their past, in their memory."

"All of Europe is a graveyard," I retorted quietly, snapping my eyes to the frail face and cloudy eyes in front of me.

"You weren't always so untrusting." She ran her finger across my palm. "A scorpion stings out of defense."

Abruptly, I retracted my hands.

"You're afraid of what I'll see?"

I was, but I didn't say so. Instead, I walked back to the altar—to the necklace, sparkling with the reflection of candlelight as if it were tempting me to reclaim it. All I had left of him had been reduced to a piece of jewelry, and, as if it housed his very spirit, it sparkled.

"He wanted you to have it," she added. "He knew you would blame yourself."

Her words gutted me. *Spof wanted you to have this.* That was all Beckham had said when he'd dropped the token in my hand outside of the hospital tent.

"Wait!" I demanded, turning back to see that she was on her way out. "What about my copper penny?"

The old woman motioned a finger to the girl.

"If you can really know these things—" I swallowed hard. "Is she upset with me? Is that why she doesn't visit?"

She looked past me with sympathetic eyes.

"Well?"

"I'm sorry, my child," she answered at last. "There's no one else with you."

Twilight Pathfinders
Ypres, Belgium, July 1918

She wore a white peasant dress the day we arrived in West Flanders to wait in reserve; my one and only conquest of the war. Every man passing through had taken notice of the Flemish farm girl with scorching copper curls pulled back in a braid—sparking our collective fantasies like wildfire as she stood posted up on the fence outside her family farm.

"Welcome to Voormezele," I said, tucking a cigarette in my lower lip. "Blink and you might miss it."

"How long are we going to be here, Lieutenant?" asked Thelander.

"Six weeks. Maybe longer."

"This seems like a *fine* farm to occupy," Mullins gawked. "What do you think?"

I followed his gaze to the redhead on the fence line, eyeing each of us dubiously as we rode in. A marvel for eyes as sore as ours.

"Something tells me the reception isn't mutual," Beckham added.

Rick nodded in agreement, turning to Mullins. "The best thing we can do for that girl is to leave her alone."

"They're right," I added, glancing her direction again. "There's no sense in forming attachments in a place like this."

Voormezele was a sleepy farming village just east of Dikkubus where we'd been lucky enough to experience our first baptism of fire since arriving in France. The locals spoke mostly Flemish and kept to themselves—seemingly determined to continue their daily routines, despite the militant presence and distant rumbles of nearby villages being shelled to pieces. From what I could see, the girl was no different.

The men, on the other hand, proved antsy and bored, unsure of what to do with their time.

"What was that for?!"

Rick and I were taking inventory one Tuesday morning when we turned around to find Private Durant surrounded by howling peers, soaked from head to toe. The girl's bucket lay on the ground at their feet, her hair blazing behind her as she stormed off toward the horse field.

"Durant!" I shouted. "What did you do?"

"Nothing, Lieutenant!"

The group of young men cowered as I walked over to them.

"Do I look fucking stupid?"

"We were just trying to get her to talk to us, sir," Private McIntire chimed in.

"Jesus Christ, what did you *say?*"

"I didn't say nothing, Lieutenant!" McIntire insisted.

"One of you better fess up, or I'll give all of you latrine duty, so help me *God*."

Private Gill opened his mouth to speak, then dropped his eyes to the pool of water, inching across the dirt.

I turned my glare on him. "Gill?"

"He asked her what color her hair was. Down there," he mumbled under his breath. "Sir."

I slapped Durant over the helmet. "For Christ's sake, we've been here a week!"

"Come on, Durant—let's go," Rick commanded.

I gritted my teeth, lifting my eyes to the sky.

"We need to keep good relations with the locals," he added, turning to me.

I squinted out to the horse pasture with a sigh.

"Miss!" I called out, hustling into the tall, grassy field. "Miss?"

She turned to face me with a hard blink, looking me over with her green, almond eyes as I approached her, winded.

"I apologize for the behavior of my private."

She nodded—a clear sign that at the very least, she understood English—so I went on, removing my hat.

"If he gives you any more trouble—or if any of them do—ask to speak with Lieutenant Thompson."

"That's you."

"Yes."

She nodded again, brushing a loose tendril from her cheek. "Thank you. Have a nice day, Lieutenant."

"You as well, Miss…"

"De Witte."

"Miss De Witte."

The group of privates were long sent away for disciplinary action by the time I returned, but the empty bucket remained where she'd dropped it.

"Crisis averted, I presume?" Rick asked, approaching me at the edge of the well.

"She didn't seem too shaken up."

"She's probably used to it. Shame." He leaned his elbow on the stone's edge, looking down into the water.

"Speak up, Rick. I can hear your thoughts from here," I said, pulling on the rope.

He let out a breathy laugh in response.

"What?" I asked, taking the overflowing pail into my hand. "I'm only de-escalating. Like you said, we need to keep good relations."

"You know what they say—the path to hell is paved with good intentions."

"No," I countered. "It's paved by Durant."

The girl's daily walk to the pasture was much further than it appeared, and I was all the gladder I'd saved her the trouble when I finally reached the finish line. She didn't notice me, bucket in hand, until I was ten feet behind her.

"Miss De Witte?"

She turned to look at me.

"I thought this was the least we owed you," I said, lifting the full bucket. "Where can I set it?"

"There is fine," she replied, motioning to the edge of the fence. Her accent was unlike anything I'd ever heard, but her English was impeccable.

A black stallion came to greet me at the fence line as I set the bucket down. I cocked an eyebrow at him curiously, then turned to her. "What's his name?" I asked, shifting my attention back to the horse.

"*Charcoal*. In your language."

I repeated the name in a hushed tone, reaching up to pet his slick muzzle. The horse turned its head, studying me inquisitively with his convex, ebony eyes as I took his nose in my other hand.

"Horses are a good judge of character," she said, observing us from the sideline.

"Ah…well, I have a feeling this one has a rebellious streak."

The girl nodded, grabbing a piece of grass by her foot. "Thank you for the water," she said, beginning to tear at it. The gnats buzzing about looked like sprites in the late afternoon sunshine, which only exaggerated her superlunary appearance. "Do you ride, Lieutenant?"

I laughed. "No."

"Would you like to learn?"

I turned to meet her gaze, questioning if I'd heard her correctly. "Sorry?"

"I could teach you," she added, allowing the shredded grass to flutter to the ground.

"I appreciate the offer, but I have a post." I turned back over my shoulder for extra emphasis. "I can't exactly leave it."

"If you change your mind, I take him out two hours before sunrise." Picking up the bucket, she averted eye contact with a smile. "Perhaps you might be a little rebellious yourself," she added, walking away.

Perhaps. I tugged on my collar, feeling suddenly warm.

For as adamantly I'd been against fraternizing, I was even quicker to ignore my own advice. The next morning, I was at the fence waiting for her.

"Now you," she'd instructed from Charcoal's mount. Offering her hand, she did what she could to help pull me up behind her.

"This is a lot higher up than I expected," I murmured.

"Here, scoot up and hold onto me."

Doing as she directed, I wrapped both arms around her tiny waist and pulled us closer together, catching a whiff of lavender from her hair.

"Are you ready, Lieutenant?"

"I am, but—" I stammered as Charcoal took a few steps forward. "There's no need to be so formal. Is there?"

"What should I call you, then?"

"Holden is fine." I peered over her shoulder as we picked up speed. "What's your name?"

"Natalia."

Lucky for me, she couldn't see the smug grin on my face, knowing how often the guys of company E had speculated over her name as they'd watched her flutter about. It was admittedly hard to not think about the fact that she was sitting between my legs, but I tried my best to listen to what she was telling me, despite the challenge at hand.

"And when you want him to pick up speed you just...move your foot like this."

"Okay..."

"Too much!" She pulled the reins, laughing. "It doesn't take much. He's a good listener."

"He and I seem to have a lot in common."

"Here you are then," she teased over her shoulder, motioning that I take the reins.

"Are you sure about that?"

"You should probably get used to it," she replied. *"You're* up front on the way back."

Clumsily, I guided us to the wood's edge. I looked around the rolling fields, layered with cool tones of blue hour as Natalia fiddled with the reins in her lap. All was quiet as far as the eye could see, with only the morning star Venus as our witness.

"This is a nice way to start the day," I remarked. "Do you come out here every morning?"

"I haven't come this far since the war broke out. It's not safe to ride by myself with things the way they are."

At last, I knew her real motive for asking me along.

"They say there's nothing left of Dibbukus," she added. "They say it's completely flattened."

The sound of artillery crackled and thundered across the sherbet horizon, causing her to flinch. I squeezed her gently from behind, and to my surprise, she leaned back onto me.

"Sound travels," I assured, resting my chin on her shoulder. "It's twenty miles from here at least." I reached for the reins in her lap but paused when she turned her cheek to me, exaggerating our proximity to one another.

"When I think of it, I'm afraid," she said lowly. "Aren't you?"

"Don't be," I whispered, delicately pecking her on the lips.

After that day, anyone with eyes could see our stolen glances when we crossed paths on the farm. She would say good morning to the group of us—to the delight of the men—just so she could talk to me. And I was no less obvious, making sure our hands touched any time I found an excuse to hand her something. We met before sunrise each morning, undeterred by the ever-nearing sound of artillery fire. It echoed its warning through the vacant pastures and cloudless summer skies. As my confidence as a rider grew, our routes became longer and our conversations more personal. We became twilight pathfinders, her and I.

Three weeks of living in the present was enough to make me forget that dreams are only dreams—eventually, you wake up.

Beckham and I were playing a game of poker with a few guys from the company when Rick joined the audience around the wobbly table.

"Screw you, Thom," said Beckham, throwing his cards down next to the lantern. "You're a goddamn bandit."

I reached for the pile of cigarettes, sticking one in my mouth. "Pay up, Fran. Ronnie."

Rick lowered his voice, leaning into my ear. "I need to talk to you."

"Where have you been all night, Spof?" asked Beckham over his shoulder.

Ronald Reith collected the cards. "Anyone up for another round?"

"I'm in," said Beckham.

Francis Cameron glanced across the table with eager eyes, hungry for my answer.

"Ante up, boys," said Ron.

He had just begun to deal when Rick leaned between us again. *"Both of you,"* he whispered sharply.

Beck turned to me.

"Be back in five," I said, tapping the table.

"What's the big idea, Spof?" Beckham scolded as he led us behind the mess tent, away from the others. "I was just—"

"Losing?"

I chuckled, lighting the cigarette in my mouth.

"Oh, spare me—I had a good feeling about this round!"

"What is it, Rick?" I asked, exhaling a breath of smoke.

"I overheard Bowen talking with the other officers tonight."

Beckham stared, bug-eyed. *"And?"*

"The 105th needs reinforcements."

I dropped my gaze.

"We're leaving as soon as Bowen gets confirmation."

"Reinforcements, huh?" Beckham stuttered.

"They're in bad shape," Rick added. "From what I could tell."

Beckham let out a dramatic sigh, shaking his head. "Well shit, I was just getting comfortable here."

"That's why I wanted to give you a heads-up."

I kept quiet, fixating my eyes on the ground. At wit's end with boredom, most of company E would be chomping at the bit to get going, but all I could think of was how I would tell *her*.

"Well," Beckham said finally, glancing back to the poker table, "I'm going to go attempt to redeem myself. Enjoy it while it lasts. Thom?"

"I'll be there in a minute," I replied.

"For the love of all that's mighty, *take your time.*"

I looked up, meeting him with a grin before he disappeared around the corner of the tent. I turned back to Rick. "Did they say when?"

"A few days if I had to guess." Rick shoved both hands in his pockets, scuffing his boot across the grass. "Should be enough time to tie up any…you know, loose ends."

He knew.

All the mornings I thought I'd snuck out unnoticed, I hadn't been stealthy enough. Rick noticed everything.

"Well, I'd better get back, too," I said.

"Wouldn't want to let them off that easy," he added.

I nodded, lifting my cigarette to see that it had nearly burnt down. "Right," I said, flicking it to the ground. "Thanks, Spof."

The following morning was a fine one, though my night had been sleepless.

Natalia knotted her fingers over my stomach, resting her chin on my shoulder as we trotted through the forest, speckled with hints of incoming dawn. A rumble reverberated through the tops of the sequoia trees—a reminder that our time together was limited and I'd soon be gone.

"It's okay," I whispered, feeling her clench onto me.

She turned her cheek, nuzzling the back of my shoulder blade. "I like being with you," she whispered back.

"I like being with you, too."

The thought of being parted from her filled me with more dread than battle itself, but I didn't know how to tell her that, or if I even should.

"Look." I motioned to a patch of bluebells up ahead. "Faery ringers."

She lifted her cheek from my shoulder as I clicked my tongue, directing Charcoal forward. As if we'd wandered into a scene from a storybook, a sea of bluebells came into view. Thousands, maybe millions of them carpeted the forest floor in every direction.

"I've never seen so many," she said.

"It's ancient woodland." Dropping the reins, I reached for her hand. "Let's stop here."

Withdrawing her arms from around my waist, she slid down Charcoal's slick coat, landing between the blooms with a thud. I did the same.

I laid my hand on her waist, crossing in front of her. "Do you know what the Irish say about bluebell woods?" I asked, tugging on her hand.

She followed, allowing me to lead her.

"They say they're enchanted." I turned back to her with a smirk. "That Fae use them to lure people into their world and trap them there."

"That doesn't sound like such a terrible fate," she said, letting go of my hand.

My smile fell flat at the sound of her wistful tone.

She gazed upon the countless flowers that surrounded us. "Perhaps there's no war."

"Nat…"

"I overheard some men in your company talking yesterday."

"The 105th needs replacements," I replied, taking her in both arms. "I know. I was going to tell you. I swear I was."

She gripped the fabric of my uniform, snuggling against my chest. "How long before you leave?"

"A few days."

She pulled away, turning her back to me.

"Nat, I'm sorry." Frustrated by words that wouldn't come, I ran my fingers over the bark of the nearest tree trunk, picking at it with my nail.

Her voice shook with trepidation as she stared ahead. "Your friend with the light hair, he said—"

"It's bad out there," I murmured, withdrawing my pocketknife. "I know." I focused my attention on the tree.

"Your leaving was inevitable," she said, cutting the silence. "Still, I—"

I turned around to see that she'd done the same. I lowered my arm. Her watery eyes slipped past me, to the carving I'd made on the trunk.

HT

+

ND

"I can't bear the thought of you hurt." The words were a mere whisper, a tremble of her bottom lip.

I kissed her.

There was no sense in forming attachments in a place like this, I'd said. But I would've crossed the ocean and done it all again without a second thought. Under a cascade of approaching daylight, she pulled me to the ground, opening for me like a peony in bloom.

I hadn't been with a woman since right before we'd boarded

the *Antigone,* and the encounter had left me wondering if I lacked the capacity for anything more than shallow lovemaking. But as our nude bodies lay facing each other atop the bed of flattened bluebells, I realized that was just another story I'd been telling myself.

"Your eyes are so beautiful," I said. "I can't decide if they're blue or green."

Her amorous, aquamarine gaze shined back at me. "They change."

I grinned, reaching for the petal caught in her red tendril.

"Do you have anyone waiting for you back home?" she asked, catching my hand as I drew away.

I measured my palm against hers, studying her fingers as she intertwined them with mine. "No, why do you ask?"

"I would feel guilty if you did."

"I don't have anyone waiting for me. At least nothing like that. Just my brother, really."

"Is he in France, too?"

"Right now he's in Italy with the Red Cross. But I figure he'll make his way back to Paris sooner or later."

"Are you scared?" She brought my hand to her lips. "You're trembling."

I ran my finger over her knuckles, managing a weak smile. "Not right now."

Natalia inched closer to me, across the violet abyss that separated us. My Aphrodite.

I brought her to my chest, wrapping my hand in her long hair. "I wish I could stay here with you forever," I whispered, resting my cheek on her forehead.

I returned to camp late that morning, leaving her in the pasture with a kiss. Making my way back across the field, I replayed the scene over and over, drawing on its solace as the birds gossiped along the wood line. I wondered what she was thinking—if it was the same as what *I* was thinking. Maybe she wondered if I would come back when this whole thing was over and done with, since I had no one waiting for me. Maybe she hoped I would. She'd all but said so, hadn't she?

I'd only just walked into our tent when Beckham burst through the flap, and I turned around to face him.

"Christ!" he exclaimed. "Where have you been?"

My eyes darted around the empty tent, confused.

"We've been looking everywhere for you! We've got to pack up—we're already behind."

Rick opened the flap and ducked in behind him. If he hadn't known what I was up to before, he certainly did now. In two seconds, he'd already assessed my disheveled hair, the sweat still stuck to my face. My partially unbuttoned collar. "We're clearing out," he said. "Just got word."

My heart sank, and I stammered, feeling my mouth go dry. "Right now?"

"It's bad, Thom," Beckham replied. "The 105th..."

I wasn't listening. I was looking at Rick, then looking past him.

"Hey! Where are you going!?"

I dashed between them, out of the tent and into the blazing sunshine. To my left, the rest of my company was starting to load up, and I mistakenly made eye contact with Pitman.

"Lieutenant—"

Before the young sergeant could finish his sentence, I was gone. I gunned it toward the farmhouse, jumping over wooden storage bins and turning the head of every soldier drinking tea and rubbing elbows on a slow morning.

With no sign of her outside, I sprinted to the side of the house, finding the nearest one-story window. Ferociously banging on the glass, I caught her just as she was walking past the parlor. "Nat!"

She rushed to the window, opening it hastily.

"Nat, I'm leaving."

"What?"

"I'm leaving," I said again, gripping the windowsill. "We're loading up now."

"You're—right *now?*"

"Yes." I stared up at her helplessly, all out of bribes for the lord of time. "I'm sorry. I…"

She softened her eyes, tracing my face with a faint smile. "I'm not."

I grabbed her cheeks with both hands. One last kiss.

Then, I reached over my head, unlatching my necklace. "Here," I whispered, plucking the warm copper penny from my tunic collar. "This was my grandfather's. Something special between him and my grandmother."

She took the penny between her fingers, leaning over so I could hook the necklace around her.

"Keep it safe for me."

Forget Me Not
Paris, January 2, 1919

"It's really coming down," Dane remarked, walking over to assess the first snowfall of the new year. Lady stood on the window ledge, possessed by the ferocious dance of flurries on the other side.

"I got more wood." I motioned to the small stack by the fireplace from my seat at the desk. "Should be enough to last us a while."

With Camille in London for the holidays, I'd sat before my new typewriter day after day, like an amnesiac in recovery. A few months into my worldly rehabilitation, I had next to no prospects other than my banished talent and military pension—which couldn't hold a penny to the kind of lifestyle she was used to. What to do with the rest of my life? That was the question.

"What are you working on over there?" asked Dane, scratching the top of Lady's head.

"I'm starting a story. Trying, anyway."

"Look at you!"

I reached into my pocket, fiddling with Rick's pendant. "It's nothing that's going to make me any money. I just wanted to write something for a friend. I don't know if I'll keep it."

"Why not?"

"I'm taking a lot of creative liberties."

"As you should." Clearing his throat, Dane walked over to the dwindling fire and began to stoke it. "Use a fictional story to tell the truth."

I turned back to my words on the page, mulling over his statement. "Extract medicine from poison," I murmured.

"Who said that? Good ole Frank, I presume?" Dane laughed to himself, wiping his sooty hand on his trousers. "I wonder how he's doing these days…surprising you didn't keep in touch when you left school, as close as you were."

"We weren't that close."

He side-eyed me, caught somewhere between confusion and amusement. "That's not how I remember it."

"Well, speaking of keeping in touch," I interjected. "Remind me to write home."

Dane rose to his feet with a triumphant smile, the fire behind him once again burning brightly. "I made sure to tell them you were alive in my last letter."

"I hope you aren't making them worry." I turned back to the window, thumbing the chain in my pocket. "Say, will you be all right if I go out for a while?"

"Well, I'm the one who keeps the fire going. So yes, I'll probably survive without you." He looked at the window. "Though I have to wonder where you'd be going."

"I need to make a delivery," I replied, grabbing two silk postcards from the desk drawer.

"For Camille?"

I nodded.

"Who's the other one for?"

"Marcie," I answered, quick to stand and grab my coat from the back of the chair. Lady jumped down from the window, following me to the door. "I'll be back in a little while," I added, allowing her to squeeze through the crack.

Lady scurried between my feet as I shuffled down the spiral staircase, mail in hand.

"You! Hold on, there!"

"Jean-Paul," I said, halting at the bottom step. "What is it?"

"*Une fille*—a girl came by asking about you!"

"Is that all?" I held up the postcards. "A little busy—"

"Le séducteur lui-même! Tu aurais dû voir son ventre!"

Just past his swung open door stood Meg, smiling at me cheerfully, as if we were the best of friends. Jean-Paul turned his head, and, horrified to see the mutual reception between me and his niece, began berating her in French, spewing orders beneath his mustache to stay away from me.

"Tell Jeanne I'm not interested," I replied, sweeping past them. "And *for Christ's sake*, Jean-Paul" —I turned back to meet his eye — "do NOT give her or any other girl a key to this building!"

I leaned into the iron door with my shoulder, pushing against the wind into the glaring white. Lady ran face first into the snow and sneezed, brushing the cold flakes from her whiskers. "You want to stay out here?" I asked, propping the door open with my foot. As if she understood, she looked up at me and blinked. "Suit yourself."

I began my walk down the freshly powdered street, listening to the crunch of the snow as folks opened their windows to stagger on balconies and children threw snowballs. One hit me in the back, followed by a boy yelling, "Pardon!" I whipped around to see a group of them taking cover behind a car. I laughed, reaching down and swiping a handful of snow. They watched with delight as I compacted it into a ball and launched it back to them playfully.

Pulling Camille's postcard from my pocket, I traced the silken embroidery as I approached the post box. I'd picked a dove holding a holly sprig for her, with *Forget Me Not* inscribed on the bottom in green thread. I'd signed it: *I miss you, my little dove.* Seven more days and she'd be home, though I was doing everything in my power not to count them.

I dropped it inside, then looked down at the second postcard in my hand.

Arriving in Montmartre after a frighteningly slippery cab ride, I exhaled a breath of relief to see that *Le Royal* was sparse, which meant I wouldn't have to wait. I was hoping for an early night, both to get home before the roads iced over and to keep me out of too much trouble. Tucking the card safely in my coat, I walked inside to thaw out.

"Look what the cat dragged in."

I looked up to see Helen and Marie Antoinette smiling down on me from the staircase. Cleopatra rushed to my side, turning her cheek for a kiss.

"Cleo. I've missed you."

She gasped at the chill of my lips. "Let me warm you up," she said, latching onto my arm.

"Afternoon, Romeo," said Marie, puffing from a long cigarette stick.

"Marie. Helen." I nodded to them both.

"Don't you want to see someone else this time?" asked Cleo.

I'd visited Vanina several times, having convinced myself that I was somehow helping her condition by supplying her income, and by some miracle, the other girls still hadn't caught on that I'd never so much as touched her. I just couldn't seem to stay away. Camille being in London had only made it worse.

"She's with the boss," Helen interjected.

"What for?"

She shrugged indifferently.

"She's been in there a while, though," Cleo added, making eyes at me. "Everyone knows Vanina is his favorite."

His favorite?

I looked around the corridor, past the chandelier to see Vanina exiting the tiny space in the back of the opium den. A stubby hand —whose only identifiable feature was a silver chain—reached from behind the curtain, grabbing her wrist. Running her delicate fingers down the tasseled edge, Vanina peeked back inside to say something.

I stood tensely; Cleo still clutched onto my arm as the melting snow began to drip through my curls. "Don't look so upset," she said.

"I'm not."

I turned from Cleo to see Vanina walking toward us, but my eyes were glued to the curtain behind her, waiting to see if the man would reveal himself.

"Holden," she said, wiping a bit of mascara from her cheek. "I didn't expect to see you. The weather is terrible."

Giving up on catching a glimpse of her keeper, I turned my full attention on her. "I didn't think you'd be so busy."

She received my tone—which had come out more accusatory than I'd initially meant—by ripping me away from Cleo. "What's the matter with you?" she snapped, pulling me up the stairs behind her.

"I should be asking you the same thing—sleeping with *the boss?*"

Vanina closed the door, sealing us in our usual room.

"I thought you'd want to see me," I argued.

"I'm not sleeping with him. He takes care of me. Me and—" She halted. "It's none of your business who I do or don't sleep with, do you understand?"

"No?"

"*No.*"

Suddenly feeling like it was very much my business, I pressed her against the back of the door, taking her face in my hands. She struggled against the kiss, slapping my face defiantly.

Her glance was ice cold as I stood there, staggered like a deer in the headlights. "You pay me to spend time with you," she said at last. "This is nothing more than that."

Reaching into my coat pocket, I pulled out the *Happy New Year* embroidered postcard, skimming my signature on the bottom.

A grateful lost soul of the rue.

"I don't know if you're fickle or just lonely," she added. "But you don't belong here."

"Neither do you," I said, flicking it onto the side table.

Kissing And Telling
Paris, January 16, 1919

It was January, all right.

If my insomnia failed in its sleep-depriving duties, the draft seeping through the window would've picked up the slack. Lady purred away, curled against my chest on the flimsy mattress as I watched the dark-blue sky melt into lilac, and the feathering cirrus clouds turn a pale orange. I tried again to close my eyes, aware that two hours of broken sleep was by no means an ideal way to start the day, but the back of my eyelids turned with carousels of pictures. "I wish I was a cat like you," I whispered, reopening them. "You sleep just fine."

A floorboard creaked, and I looked over to see Dane. "Sorry," he said. "I was trying to be quiet."

"Don't worry." I crossed my arms, flopping onto my back. "I was already awake."

Tired of cuddling with me, Lady perked her head up and stretched her paws across my chest before hopping off the mattress to go see Dane.

"Turncoat," I called after her.

"You know, we can reschedule tonight if you're not feeling up to it," said Dane.

I sat up, feeling the weight of my bedhead as I stared him down. "You mean if *you're* not feeling up to it?"

"You didn't get any sleep."

"What else is new?" I laughed under my breath, grabbing my pack of cigarettes from the floor. "Just admit it—you don't want to go."

"All right," he said, shooting me a miserable look. "I don't want to go."

"Why not? It'll be a good time, and she's pretty—Marge. And kind of shy, like you." I struck a match, lighting the end of the cigarette. "Plus, I promised Camille that the four of us could go out. She doesn't want Marge to feel neglected while she's visiting."

"We're all feeling neglected," he teased. "You've seen Camille every day since she's been back."

"She's good for me." My chest stirred with butterflies. "Don't you think so?"

He walked into the kitchen with Lady on his heels as I hinged on his opinion, which he took forever to share. "She's looking for someone to settle down with," he said finally, reaching for the milk in the ice box.

"I think I am, too."

My comment caused Dane to pause, and Lady gaped at him with pleading eyes, waiting impatiently for him to fill her saucer. When he finally spoke, his tone was almost suspicious. "Really."

I laid back, feeling particularly idealistic as I exhaled a stream of smoke from my worn-out lungs. "She makes me feel young again."

"You are young."

"No," I replied. "We're all old men here."

He nodded, looking absorbed in a thought he wasn't willing to share. "So, if Marge asks me about—"

"You'll come, then?" I asked, grinning smugly.

. . .

It was sunny but cold when we set out for the Saturday market. Heaps of muddy snow piled every corner, melting into the puddles of violet dye from vendors trying to color their flowers. It was a beautiful sight, truly, but I was glad I'd left my nice shoes at home.

"I have to ask," started Dane, as we turned the corner. The noisy street was rife with beggars. "Why the change of heart?"

Among the commotion of vendors haggling and locals commiserating, I caught my eye on an unfortunate fellow leaning against a building on the left. I didn't flinch at the sight of his missing leg, having gotten used to the sight of amputated limbs, but I did feel a pang of guilt, knowing it could just as easily have been me in his place, taking donations in a rusted tin cup.

"Is it really so surprising that I'd want to settle down?" I asked, turning my pockets inside out, hoping I had something to give him.

"I thought you were more interested in temporary conquests," Dane replied.

"I've always wanted a family. You know that."

"You'd have to...you know" —he shrugged— "learn to stick with one woman."

I grinned, jiggling a few coins in my hand. "How hard could it be?"

Diverting from our path, I stepped out of the stream of market-goers and dropped them into the expat's cup, leaving him with a nod.

"What do you think about it?" I asked, rejoining Dane. "About her and me."

"What does it matter what I think?"

I stopped to examine a cart of used books, and he did the same. "I value your opinion."

He ran his fingers atop the spines. "I think she's great."

"Don't sound so glum," I poked, grabbing one. I scanned the title—*Les Liaisons dangereuses*—then turned my attention back to Dane. "We'll have a swell time tonight, just you wait…"

He looked up to see me gawking at a black babushka in the produce line a few yards away. "Who is that?" he asked.

"I'll be right back," I promised, absently handing him the book.

I hadn't seen Vanina since our quarrel a few weeks ago when I'd trudged home in the snow under the fast-approaching night sky. Stealing up from behind, I tapped her once on the shoulder.

"I know you probably don't want to talk to me, but I couldn't not say hello," I said.

It was evident from the way her eyes widened and her lips separated that I was the last person she thought she'd run across that morning, but she didn't look *entirely* disappointed to see me. "Do you...live close by?"

As I opened my mouth to speak, a little girl with a babushka of her own peeked out at me from behind Vanina's skirt.

"Around the corner," I replied, gaping at the miniature. Had I known she was a mother, I would've paid her more.

"This is Emma," she said.

"Hi there." I knelt, greeting the pair of chocolate brown eyes with a gentle smile. "How old are you?"

The little girl held up her fingers.

"Four!"

She smiled bashfully.

I followed the length of Vanina's skirt, squinting up at her silhouette against the blinding sun. "Are you two going to be here awhile?" I asked.

"We're about finished."

"Well—can I walk you?" I stood up and brushed my pants. "I'd just like to try and make up for last time we saw each other. If you'd let me."

Dane shot me a confused look across the crowd as I made my way back over to him. "Is that her?" he asked. He wasn't stupid.

"Yeah," I confirmed. "That's her."

"Is that her daughter?"

I nodded. He gave me a stern glare—the kind a parent would give a child about to touch something they weren't supposed to.

"I'm going to walk them home," I added innocently.

"What about Camille?"

"I won't be long," I promised.

Vanina didn't say much as we sloshed through the wintery streets with Emma between us, not that I expected her to. I was used to leading the conversation.

"I'm glad I ran into you."

"Why is that?"

"So I can properly apologize. You were right—it was none of my business."

"And *you* were wrong," she replied, turning to me.

"I didn't know." I motioned to Emma. "I mean, I wouldn't have guessed it."

"Mama," whined the girl, tugging Vanina's hand. "I'm tired."

Vanina paused to look down at her. "Just a little longer. We're almost there."

"But I'm…"

Her lower lip quivered, and my heart melted, joining the snow puddle at my feet. "I could carry her," I offered.

"You really don't have—"

Emma sighed in relief as I scooped her up, wrapping her arms gingerly around my neck.

I couldn't help but wonder what the other street goers thought of us. A child with her parents, perhaps? Maybe nothing at all. Maybe it was only me who speculated over the life stories of people I passed on the sidewalk.

"I'll admit, I'm happy to see you, too," said Vanina, slowing to a stop.

I grinned at her, readjusting the sleepy child in my arms before handing her off to her mother.

"It's nice to end things on a better note," she added.

Nodding, I tucked my hands in my coat pockets and looked

up at the dilapidated duplex. Vanina hugged onto Emma, hiding behind her shoulder.

"You're right," I said finally. "There's no reason it should end on a bad one."

Interrupted by the sound of the neighbor's door swinging open, I turned to see a stout, gray-haired woman walk outside, broom in hand.

Vanina shifted Emma, lifting a hand to wave. "Bonjour, Miss Helene."

She smiled cheerily in response, narrowing her eyes at me before she turned her attention to sweeping her stoop.

"Well," I mumbled. "I guess I'll—"

But Vanina was already unlocking the door and slipping through the opening with Emma on her hip.

Marge was painfully quiet, overly hesitant and by all accounts a terrible match for my brother. She had a knack for locating the clock in every establishment, and I could tell by the way she dragged her feet that she'd been just as conned into this outing as Dane—though, he seemed happy enough to be in the vicinity of Camille. It was only when I suggested we see a film after dinner that Marge perked up and the mood lifted.

The girls wanted a romance, so we settled on *J'acusse*, a postwar drama centered around a pair of troubled soldiers within a love triangle. If it hadn't been so close to home, I might've enjoyed it more.

"Well, *that* was a relaxing two hours," I mumbled, holding the door for Camille.

Hot in conversation, the crowd poured out beneath the theater lights, discussing the film amongst themselves.

"Poor Edith," Marge added.

Dane followed close behind her. "It was certainly culturally relevant," he said.

"Did you like it?" she asked, slowing her pace.

"Very much."

"Poor Edith—poor *Jean,*" I countered, catching up with the group. "I don't have to understand French to know that the poor man was driven mad."

Camille tugged on my hand eagerly as we stepped onto the cobblestone, sparkling in her winter dress with eyes to match. "Did you find his experience relatable at all?"

I laughed, pulling her in close. "I know all too well what it's like to tear up your own writing."

"No," she gasped. "You wouldn't!"

"Oh—he would," said Dane.

Camille and I looked over our shoulders simultaneously to find Marge's arm in his, then turned to each other with triumphant smiles.

"What shall we do now?" Camille asked. "Any ideas?"

"No ideas," Dane answered. "But somewhere warmer, preferably," he added with a shiver.

"Let's play the law of surprise," I suggested. "We'll walk and see what we discover."

"Marge?"

Camille turned around to gauge her cousin's reaction, and I followed, only to see that Marge and Dane were chatting away about cinema."The law of surprise it is," she added, pulling me forward.

"Good," I said. "It's much too early to say goodnight."

With a sugary grin, she grabbed the edges of my coat, wrapping herself within it. Dane was only right to interject, or we might've forgotten anyone else was there.

"So wait, where are we going?"

"Holden suggested we leave it to the law of—" Camille jumped as a car rounded the empty corner, letting off a raucous *pop*.

The sound bounced from wall to wall, reverberating through the empty streets. I let go of her, thinking my heart might combust from how fast it was racing. I was back in St. Quentin, my hands still warm and slippery from the insides of a young sergeant.

"Holden! It was just a—"

Feeling someone grip my shirt, I swung as hard as I could. I'd meant to do it again until a splitting scream snapped me out of it.

"*Stop!* Stop it!"

"Beck—I'm sorry," I stammered.

"*Beck?*"

Of course, it was him who'd found me next to Thelander's body. But it was *Dane* gushing blood when I came to. The law of surprise indeed.

Mortified, I could hardly speak. "Dane, I..." I stuttered, feeling the panic set in. He wiped his nose with the back of his hand. "I... I didn't hurt you, did I?"

No one spoke.

I turned to both girls, whose eyes glinted with frightful shock, then glanced down at my knuckles, spattered with his blood. "Fuck! What did I do?"

"I'm okay," Dane assured. Camille ran to his aid, handing him her handkerchief to stop the bleeding, and I turned away, feeling like I might be sick. "It's okay," he reiterated calmly. "I shouldn't have grabbed you."

I didn't stick around long enough to see what anyone else had to say about it.

"Holden!" Camille reached for my hand, but I yanked it away. "Holden, wait!" I walked briskly, ignoring her. "Where are you going?" she pleaded.

"Home. If you know what's good for you, you'll do the same."

"Don't be that way! Let me walk with you, at least?"

"Don't you understand?"

She tucked her hair behind her ear, nervous, opening her mouth to speak, but I plowed ahead.

"I'm like Jean! I've got my own army of the dead—just like the film. They haunt me whenever they see fit."

"But Holden, that's *fictional*. It's a story!"

"To you," I muttered. "It's fictional to you." The mist in my eyes dissipated as I stared down at the wet cobblestone, washed in light from the waning gibbous moon.

"I didn't realize," she said finally. "You hide it so well. I forget how you've suffered."

"Wouldn't you?"

Camille was silent.

"You can go," I said, turning away from her. "I'll get home fine."

"If that's what you want."

It wasn't. Alone was the last thing I wanted to be, but I wouldn't admit it.

"Or," she added, approaching me, "we could leave Dane and Marge to fend for themselves." Her cheeky smile was contagious. "I think they were hitting it off. It'd be a shame if I ruined it."

"You're right," I agreed, reaching for her hand. "It would."

I couldn't tell if Camille was intrigued, repulsed or some cocktail of the two as I led her through the squalor of the 5th arrondissement. Surely she would've never been caught dead on this side of town, especially at night, but if she was frightened, she didn't show it.

"You get used to it," I assured as we stepped over the hand of an unconscious body, sprawled across rue du Cardinale Lemoine. Knowing the poor sap would freeze to death, I turned back, pulling him out of the snow and into the slouching position. "Believe it or not, it's quite charming in the daytime," I added.

"Is this where you live?"

"Our little slice of paradise." I pointed to the downstairs window, packed with people on the other side. "There's the dance hall. It's a bit seedy, but it can be fun, and over there—"

"Oh!" Camille gasped.

"Ah—and my favorite part of all." Lady mewed as I scooped her up, slipping her into my coat collar. *"There you are,"* I scolded. "I've been looking all afternoon for you."

Camille ogled at the sight of the kitten tucked snuggly against my neck. "Oh, *Holden.*"

"This is Lady MacBeth," I said, stepping closer to her. "My little smudge of good luck."

"I adore her," Camille cooed, scratching her tuffs of black fur. "Wherever did you find such a precious kitty?"

"She found me."

She lowered her voice, tilting her head as she cozied up to me. "Listen. She's purring."

"She likes you. I can tell."

Removing her fingers, Camille cupped her hands around her mouth, trying to thaw them with her breath.

"Do you want me to call you a cab?" I asked. "You'll catch a cold, and it'll be my fault."

She glanced from Lady to me, eyes glistening. "I'm sure it would be just as warm inside."

It was easy to imagine, in vivid detail, what might occur once we were alone, but as we walked up the spiral staircase together, I wondered how I'd manage.

"Brace yourself," I warned as I unlocked the door to our run down flat. "I know it's not what you're used to."

Lady jumped from my coat, scurrying in, and I turned to Camille, who was illuminated beautifully by the city lights leaking through the window. She leaned in the doorway with a coy grin, paying no attention to the state of our bachelor pad. Her eyes were on me.

I led her in by the hand, closing the door behind us. We were about to sleep together, and I'd never felt worse about myself.

"How would you set the scene, now?" she asked, brushing a stray hair from my forehead.

My answer was a quick kiss, then a longer one. We threw off our coats. I slid my hands into her ashy hair, guiding her lips open with my tongue. There was a serenity to her touch that tempered my hot-blooded inclinations, leaving me feeling timorous and clumsy—an enchanter without his charms.

She reached for my belt.

"Wait," I murmured in between her dewy kisses. "Camille." I felt the leather around my waist tug as she started unbuckling it. "*Stop.*" I grabbed her hands. "Please."

She drew back with a palpable confusion.

"No, no—" I whispered, reaching for her. "I didn't mean that."

Averting her gaze, she tucked her hair behind her ear, pulling the strap of her dress back over her shoulder.

"Sometimes I..." The ten seconds of silence that followed lagged insufferably, and I bit the inside of my cheek, feeling them turn hot. It was coming out all wrong. "I'm just wound up from earlier. That's all."

"I thought you..."

"I do," I whispered back.

"Your heart." She laid her palm on my chest. "It's racing."

"I'm afraid," I admitted, catching the words in my throat.

Camille ran her fingertips over my lips, then wrapped both arms around my neck in a tight coil. She surrendered to the repentant brush of my lips on her shoulder, then her mouth. I finished unfastening my belt, and she kneeled in devotion, my hands finding her hair, neck, the tie of her dress. I lifted her back to me, shedding layers to the floor until there was nothing but bone.

Afterward, we lay awake, steeping in a euphoric bliss with my cheek to her chest. I squeezed her gently, closing my eyes as she ran her fingers through my damp waves. Rising up and down with the rhythm of her breath, I listened to the soft percussion of her heartbeat as midnight melted into morning.

Her hazel eyes held a constellation of glowing gold freckles, and they were the first thing I saw when I opened mine the following morning. Tangled together in a pile of blankets, with Lady curled up at our feet, Camille turned to me with a whisper.

"If she comes up missing, it wasn't me."

"She has a way of stealing your heart, doesn't she?" I asked.

Readjusting herself, Camille pulled the blanket over our heads with a sweet grin. "Good morning, ma chérie," she said, tucking a piece of hair behind my ear.

I lifted the deflating blanket valley between us with a sheepish smile, taking a moment to study her eyes. "Good morning."

"Sleep well?"

"Like a baby," I said, shifting so that she was beneath me. "You'll have to forgive me for all the ways I might ruin this."

Her brow wrinkled.

"I'm afraid I will," I confessed. "I'm not used to be so taken with someone."

She pursed her lips and turned her cheek—as if she were trying to conceal the smile that I'd coaxed out of her. I nuzzled her just below her ear.

"No tickling."

"Okay," I whispered back, running my fingers over her temples, unprepared for the suggestive grin that she gave me. "We'll have to be quiet," I hushed, kissing her bottom lip.

Interrupted by the sound of Dane's bedroom door swinging open, I emerged from our cocoon to greet his bruised face. He must've walked in after we'd fallen asleep last night. Nestled next to Camille, I hadn't even stirred. She followed my lead, pulling the covers down to reveal her smiling eyes.

"Sorry, I'm just getting something to eat," he said, shuffling past us.

Now I *really* regretted not taking the bedroom.

"Quite all right—I was just leaving," Camille replied, ducking under the edge of the blanket.

I felt a twinge of panic as I held her in my arms, aware that our night together was quickly slipping into the past. "Do you really have to go so soon?" I asked, snuggling closer until I was nose to nose with her on the pillow. I eyed her hopefully, tracing the ring of fire in her irises. "We could spend the day together…feed more pigeons," I suggested, running my finger over her shoulder. "What do you say?"

"I want to," she assured. "But…"

I forced a grin, trying to conceal the weight of my disappointment.

"I didn't come home last night. I wouldn't want to worry my parents any more than I already have."

"Of course," I said, clearing my throat. "I'll walk you out, then?"

Pinching my cheek, she pecked me on the lips and sat up, clutching the blankets tightly to her chest. *"Dane,"* she called out, "stay in there for a moment, would you?"

We dressed swiftly, and grabbing her coat on our way out, she peered into the kitchen to find Dane munching on a piece of bread. The two of them held a mutual gaze just long enough for me to notice, and then Camille spoke. "Did you see that my cousin got home last night?"

Dane nodded, and I studied him as he reached for the glass of milk on the counter. "We ended up seeing another film," he said.

"Oh! C'est bien."

"Oui."

"Well," she said warmly, turning back to me at the door, "I hope you have a nice day."

"You, too," he replied, mid chew.

We walked down the staircase hand in hand, and I marveled at how different I felt—we felt—since we'd last climbed them. Camille nodded hello to Jean-Paul as he gathered his mail just outside of his door, and I shot him a glare from behind her, warning him to keep his mouth shut.

"You were right," she joked, hugging onto me as we sloshed through the snow caps in the winter sunshine. "It's much more charming in the daytime."

"I'm glad you were here to witness its charm. Though I'm not sure your parents would agree."

"Nonsense." She whipped around to face me, poking my chest with her pointer finger. "They're dying to meet the handsome American captain they keep hearing so much about."

"I could always come with you," I proposed. "We could have lunch with them."

"A planned dinner might be better," she said, grabbing the edges of my coat. "Give you both a bit of time to prepare, you know?"

"Okay, dinner then."

My eyes scanned the roads for a cab, and I rubbed the back of my neck, sorry I'd suggested it. *Meet her parents*—I might as well have dropped to my knees and begged her not to leave.

"Hey," she cooed, looking up at me. "We'll see each other soon."

"We'll see each other tomorrow," I declared.

She grinned, taking my cheeks in her hands. "Tomorrow and the next day."

Dane had yet to move from his spot in the kitchen when I returned, and before I'd even shut the door behind me, he was ready to pounce. "You can't run off on me anymore when that happens," he scolded. "I thought we'd reached an understanding on that?"

"I know," I said, pinching the bridge of my nose. "I'm sorry about all of it." I motioned to his face. "Especially that."

Based on how quickly his tone shifted, I must've looked as morose as I felt. "I feel like you should be in a better mood, considering," he added.

I walked to the windowsill and started picking at its chipped paint. "Did you have a good time with Marge?"

"Sure." He hesitated. "From the looks of it, it seems like your night was redeemed."

"Yeah." Reaching for the pack of cigarettes next to the Royal, my mind raced back to how vulnerable I'd felt with her. "It's too bad it can't last," I added, striking a match to burn it away. "The closeness you feel after making love."

"I thought you didn't kiss and tell," he said, motioning for the pack.

"It's nothing you didn't already know," I replied, tossing it to him reluctantly. "I don't mean to rub it in." I could see I'd struck a nerve, despite his best attempts to hide it. "I know you're fond of her," I added. "I can tell."

Dane turned his attention to the window.

"Anyway, she seemed pretty eager to leave."

He laughed a little. "Because she needed to get home?"

I wandered over and plopped down on the edge of my mattress, allowing the cigarette to lay limply on my lip. I knew all too well what leaving early really meant.

"You can't tell me you're upset over that…"

I shrugged.

"Not everyone is you," he added, reading my mind.

"Still." I leaned over to pet Lady, who'd jumped up next to me. "I should end it before I get too caught up."

Dane reached for a tiny book sitting near my typewriter—the one I'd given him at the market. He licked his thumb, flipping to a page. "Don't give her the runaround, Holden," he murmured, blowing a stream of thoughtful smoke. "If you're looking for a reason to end it, make it an honest one."

A Proper Catholic
Paris, January 21, 1919

Camille and my promise to see each other melted away with the snowcaps outside. While I'd admittedly made no moves myself, the silence on her end had me convinced she wanted nothing to do with me. But who could fault her for it? It was bad enough that I couldn't escape my issues—why should I condemn her to an equal fate?

Truth be told, I wasn't in any place to see her anyway. The neurosis from my shellshock episode had lingered like mustard gas on a dewy summer morning, and again, I'd found myself in the slippery labyrinth of the faeries, having forgotten to leave a trail of breadcrumbs to find my way back. Anxious and fidgety, all I could do was hyper focus on something else.

"Sorry to interrupt your divine frenzy, but I'm heading out," said Dane, appearing at my side.

I halted my furious typing, flicking my cigarette over the full ashtray as he read over my shoulder.

"The Captain and the Reckoner."

"It's a short story," I said, looking up at him.

"Let me see it."

"I don't let anyone read my writing."

"Since when?"

"Since before I left school." I snatched the story from the Royal and slipped it under the neighboring pile of blank paper. "Sorry," I added, softening my tone. "It's just not finished."

"I like the title. How'd you come up with it?"

"It was a captain's nickname in the 108th."

We stared at each other for a few seconds before he grinned faintly and murmured, "The Reckoner? Quite a nickname."

I slumped down in my chair, dropping my eyes back to the keys.

"Maybe you should try and go outside later," he added.

"I might just stay here and keep going." I pointed to the Royal. "You know how it is—when it flows, it flows."

"You can't stay cooped up in here forever." His voice was gentle like our father's, and so was his touch, when he laid his hand on my shoulder. "Have you heard from her?"

"No," I replied swiftly, cutting the air like a knife. I hadn't slept a wink since she'd been there last—or left the apartment in equally as long. I had no appetite, couldn't sit still, and my fantasies of a French cottage by the sea with our three hypothetical children was only the cherry on top. "But you're right," I added, changing the subject. "I'll try to go out later."

He smirked, plucking the lit cigarette from my mouth. "Eat something while you're at it," he ordered, putting it out. "Wine doesn't count."

I kept my word to Dane, even if it was almost three o'clock before I mustered the courage to walk down the street. But not knowing where to go or what to do, coupled with the anxiety of another flashback, my grand journey ended just a few blocks from home on the steps of Saint-Étienne-du-Mont.

Fiddling with Rick's pendant in one hand and cigarette in the other, I noted the long faces of a few elderly female patrons as they climbed the stairs. I considered following them inside— perhaps finding a home in the back row where I could contemplate *God's plan* like a proper Catholic. Maybe they would even strike up a conversation with the young stranger sitting all alone, and I'd confess my troubles to a few well-meaning grandmothers.

Reluctantly, I eyed the entry doors from over my shoulder.

The women said nothing to me as I held the tall, wooden door for them on their way out. Peeking past them, there seemed to be only one other person in the sanctuary—a man sitting in front, gazing into the abyss of votive candles. I took my time as I walked the length of the aisle, taking a seat on the opposite side. Only a few minutes later, my unpredictable cough ripped through the silent church, refusing to be stifled.

"Gas?"

Turning left, I met the raspy American accent of the gentleman across the way. "Flu," I replied, mid-cough. I glanced down to his amputated leg, then back to his eyes. "Where'd you lose it?"

"St. Quentin Canal." He shifted to face me, wrapping his arm around the neighboring chair. "I remember your face. From the other day."

"The marketplace," I muttered, remembering how I'd mined my pockets for something to give the wary veteran.

"Who were you with at St. Quentin?" I asked. "I was there with the 108th."

"I was a Lieutenant with the 119th. Taylor is my name."

"No shit." I moved a few seats closer to him. "The 119th—we were at Camp Wadsworth together."

A smile graced his rugged face, and I motioned for him to take his time, seeing that he was having trouble speaking. "South Carolina," he managed finally. "Since the day I was born."

"We're almost neighbors. I'm from Virginia."

"108th is New York National Guard, isn't it?"

I nodded, leaning my elbows on my knees across the aisle. "I was studying at Princeton when I joined up."

"You're smart, then."

I grinned. "I certainly thought so."

Taylor winced as he shifted again to a more comfortable position. "But not smart enough to stay away from this miserable war."

"No," I replied. "I traded in a bad situation for an even worse one. Of course, I didn't know that at the time. I just wanted out."

"I wanted adventure." He paused to catch his breath. "I wanted adventure, and I got it."

My mind slid back to the New York City parade. To the stiff, new uniforms. Pockets stuffed with candy. "The idea of going to war with a group of friends was enthralling to me, too," I said quietly. "Then they all died."

"Aren't they the lucky ones, then," he wheezed. "You won't catch anyone here praying for the living."

"I don't know if I'd call them lucky," I replied, blinking hard. I could envision the fields of St. Quentin ablaze in the dozens of dancing flames on the altar. The smell of flesh still lingered in my nose. "A vertical victory counts for something. The fact that we're still standing."

"Barley," he reminded me. "And that's easy to say when you have both of your legs."

"Maybe. But it doesn't make them lucky that you come here and pray for them. It just makes them dead."

"*I come here* because it's cold outside."

I lifted my chin, studying closer the grimy clothes and paper-thin coat of another faithless man, much like myself. "I'm here because I was afraid to walk any further," I admitted. "Loud noises set me off."

"Then it's crossed your mind, too. The alternative."

Without having to ask, I knew what alternative he was referring to. I faced forward in the chair, crossing my arms over my chest.

"It doesn't matter if we believe or not," he added. "None of us will see heaven." Tired from the conversation, I grew silent.

"Thank you," Taylor said at last. "For the other day."

I turned to him, knowing my only protection from a similar fate had been pure chance. "Do you need any more?"

"Too much charity makes a man feel worse."

I stood up and unfasted the buttons on my chest, stepping center aisle. "How about a coat then?" I asked, folding it over my arm. "We look about the same size, and I have another at home."

"I manage fine."

He eyed me incredulously as I approached him, opening the coat and laying it across his shoulders as if I were tucking a child in at bedtime. "You do." I nodded reassuringly to his teary brown eyes, in the same way Eldred Carter had done for me. "Take care, brother," I whispered.

REVELATIONS
RONSSOY, FRANCE, OCTOBER 1918

HOLDING my lit cigarette between my teeth, I stood from my roost at the quarry's edge as the rest of the officers discussed business as usual below. I was half a pack down since I'd managed to slip away, but they'd done nothing to relieve my stress over going back. There were still more tunnels to clear, and two days of company 'rest' had looked more like distracted reading and constant pacing in a place too suspiciously quiet to sleep.

"Might I have a word?"

I turned away from Rick's voice, plucking the cigarette from my mouth and flicking it down into the quarry; I watched as the cherry bounced against the rocks on the way down. "What can I do for you, Lieutenant."

"All set for tomorrow," he replied.

I nodded, turning my attention to the dark horizon line.

"You've hardly spoken to me since we got back," Rick huffed, scraping his boots across the rock ledge.

I met his eye earnestly. "Sometimes there's nothing to say."

"Horseshit." He took a seat on the edge of the cliff, dangling one leg.

I did the same, dropping my eyes to the speckled campfires below.

"I've never known you to lack the words," he added.

"Nothing would've made me happier than blowing a hole through his skull," I murmured, holding my pack of cigarettes to my mouth and grabbing another with my teeth. "Maybe I would feel better if I had." I could feel Rick's eyes on me as I struck a match, illuminating the inside of my cupped hand—still bandaged.

"Something came over you out there. I saw it and so did Beck."

"Spare me your sermon, Rick," I said, blowing smoke. "I'm not in the mood."

"I'm only saying that you did the right thing."

"What's it matter anymore?" I wiped my eye with the back of my hand, hoping he didn't notice under the starlight. "We're no better than animals here."

"No. But you kept your humanity another day."

I picked up a rock, chucking it across the quarry. "All thanks to you."

A FEW DAYS PRIOR————————

"Here they come—what'd I say? God bless the Aussies!"

Out of breath, I followed Spofford's voice, peering over the fortified German trench to see the 3rd Australian Infantry running toward us. God bless the fucking Aussies.

The plan had been simple on paper. The 108th had one main objective: take St. Quentin Canal. But hours of shelling beforehand had scrambled our brains like eggs, and by the time the assault had begun, Death himself was a welcomed respite from the claustrophobic trench walls. It was a miracle we were still standing, and an even bigger miracle that we'd managed to hold the enemy trench on our own for over an hour. The morning had been a bloodbath. But there was no time to share stories—the clock was ticking, and men were dying.

"Make room!" I ordered, shuffling a few corpses against the wall to make way for incoming infantry.

"Move along, fellas!" Beckham ordered.

"Welcome to our humble abode!" I shouted up to the Aussie captain, who slid down into the trench. "Make yourself at home."

"You're the first American officer I've seen since Pitmanemont," he said, eying the blood splattered shotgun slung over my arm.

I reached for a pack of cigarettes in the pocket of one of the dead, pulling one out and sticking it between my lips. "Captain Holden Thompson, 108th infantry." I extended my hand.

"James Black," he replied, shaking quickly.

I motioned to the trench wall, moving over so he could get a better look through the peephole at the foggy greenish hue creeping toward our line. "Quennemont Farm is the objective from here," I said, striking a match.

"What do you see?" asked Beckham to my right.

I took a long drag. "Chlorine." I turned to Black, snubbing the rest of the cigarette on the trench wall. "Tell your men to secure gas masks."

I could hear Beckham and Spofford echo my order over a backdrop of artillery as I pushed through the horde, packed tight as sardines. Men reached for last cigarettes, some for photos of sweethearts. I steadied myself with my hand on the wall. I inhaled. I exhaled, focusing on the texture of the wood beneath my fingers.

"Sir?"

Thelander looked me over like he knew I needed a moment. He was an observant kid.

"Where's your mask, Thelander?" I asked. "Fuck's sake, do you want to be crying for the next week?"

"I don't have one," he admitted. "Someone knocked it right off me—I didn't even realize it was gone."

"Now you do," I replied, tossing him mine. "I'll find one on the field."

"Sir, I—"

I grabbed him by both shoulders, eyeing him sternly. "That's an order, Victor," I added, softening my tone.

He nodded reluctantly, the mask limp in his hand.

I made my way back to Beckham and Spofford, who awaited direction at the front with Black and a few of his lieutenants. "Are we ready?" I asked, digging in my pockets.

Beckham narrowed his eyes on me, dropping his voice to a sharp whisper. "Where's your mask?"

I motioned to the handkerchief I'd pulled out of my pocket. "I'm in the market for a new one."

"You can't be serious—what if they start throwing yellow shells?"

"They won't use mustard gas," I replied. "It would pollute their counterattack."

"You're so sure they'll counterattack?"

I turned my attention to the Aussie captain, whose voice was stifled through the heavy breathing of his respirator.

"The idea is that we're going to make them," I replied, patting his shoulder.

Rick nodded to me, kissing his pendant before tucking it into his collar.

Jumping over the top first, the rest of Company E fell in directly behind me. All was quiet against the battered, soulless landscape. The empty eye socket of a bloated body watched as I drenched my handkerchief in a nearby crater of tepid, bloody rainwater.

I'd just returned the soggy cloth to my face when a bullet ripped through an American private in the front. Six more men fell like bowling pins—then seven, then thirteen—I couldn't tell who. I glanced up from my scope to see Pitman struggling to get the arm of a wounded sergeant around his neck, but I lost sight of them when a shell landed at my feet, blasting me with tear gas. When I lifted my stinging lids, Pitman was on his back. His right eyepiece was shot through, splattering the inside of his mask with a vibrant red. Without a doubt I knew that his soul—whatever it is a *soul* might be—had left before he'd ever hit the ground. The anonymous sergeant lay next to him, with both arms around his neck in a thankful embrace.

As the sun rose higher, we were too blinded by the reflective smog to fire back with any accuracy. There were no inlays, no trees to take cover behind, only fence posts and webs of tangled barbed wire, waiting for prey. A shell exploded nearby, eliciting a ghastly shriek. My ears rang and my vision blurred, but I could hear Rick shouting, and I could feel myself falling. I hit the ground.

Gripping the grass, I felt someone topple over me as dirt rained from the sky and the earth shook beneath.

"Beckham! Thompson!"

"We're all right, Spof!"

Beckham lifted himself off and pulled me to my feet as Rick ran over to us, passing Mullin's helmet on the ground. The shell had missed me by a hair, spraying my tunic with the dusty, glittering blood of our friend.

I never thought to say goodbye that morning.

More chlorine gas shells flew overhead, streaking the haze with fresh trails of smoke. I kicked one like a Princeton football, launching the flaming coal back at the masked German infantry, who'd sprouted from the ground like poppies. We charged each other like rabid dogs, eager to tear each other to pieces.

I grabbed my knife, embedding it between the neck and shoulder of the man in front of me. He fell to the ground, taking me down with him. Another knocked my knife from my hand, climbing on top of me. I writhed, gasping for air under the weight of my concealed assailant. I could see the grayish hue of his eyes through his goggles, and for a split second, the feral gaze in them disappeared. It was as if he'd suddenly realized that I was a human being, and he was about to end my life—extinguishing every memory I'd ever had. The man blinked hard, as if to say *I'm sorry*.

I shut my eyes in violent anticipation as the point of his dagger struck with a thud against the chest pocket of my uniform. It seemed the only thing that had separated me from a bloody end was *Die Leiden des jungen Werthers*, bookmarked with the portrait of a dead man's baby. Wrestling for the knife, I grabbed the blade with my palm, headbutting him so hard I was sure I'd cracked my skull. I didn't hesitate when he lost his grip.

When I awoke, it was to the crackling of burning timber.

Cinders wafted across an ironic blue sky as I lay below, still gripping the blade, now glued to my hand with blood. I wiggled out from beneath the corpse, pushing him aside. Wincing, I dropped the knife, stretching my hand to access the damage. After a few futile attempts to blow the dirt from my wound, I reached for a bandage in my pocket, tying it around my hand. Pulling off the man's mask, I rose to a kneeling position, nauseous.

Thick, black smoke had cascaded across the battlefield, engulfing my surroundings in an opaque cloak. From the pileup of bodies that surrounded me, it was clear that I'd been out for a while. Long enough for the sound of gunfire to become distant.

My head was pounding. I needed to go.

I checked my shotgun, pistol and what limited ammo I had left in my cartridge, looping my knife in my belt as well as the German's. Then, struggling to find my balance, I wobbled to my feet with the grace of a seasick sailor.

A tree branch snapped.

My hand reached for my pistol instinctively. My eyes blinked in disbelief. But it was no delusion or result of my concussion. A horse anxiously paced the ignited wood line, a fairytale white against charred smoke, a sight that would make even the best writer grapple for his words. In the stirrup, the foot of a dead German officer.

Shoving the gas mask in my knapsack, I stepped closer, feeling the heat of the inferno touch my face. "Don't kick me," I murmured, holding both hands up. "Please."

It was clear from his body language that this horse was no farm friendly Charcoal, and the way he scuffed his hooves on the ground was enough to remind me of my experience level. Still, keeping my hands visible, I shifted to the side and reached for the boot of the officer, tangled in the stirrup. The body fell to the ground with a thud.

Another snap. A burning branch came crashing down, which did little in my efforts to calm the horse. I reached to touch his coat, speckled with soot and blood.

"Shhhh."

The horse blinked at me warily, but he didn't buck as I walked around front and cautiously reached for the reins. "There," I said, taking hold of them. "We're allies now."

"HALT!"

I pursed my lips.

"Halt!" barked the voice again.

Transferring the reins to one hand, I raised the other, lifting my eyes. Two German lieutenants stood on the offensive.

"Don't make any moves," warned a third voice over my shoulder.

"Ich gebe auf," I replied.

"Du spricht Deutsch." One of the lieutenants grinned, his fingers hovering dangerously over his holster. "Go on then," he said, nodding to my other hand. "Hands up."

Before he could grab his gun, the German knife from my belt loop was sticking out of his chest. The second lieutenant fired a shot, causing the horse to rear in panic. Someone's arms wrapped around my neck. Death-gripping the reins in one hand and reaching behind me with the other, I seized the German's saber, shoving my boot in the stirrup and jumping onto the horse's back.

Then, as if she were whispering in my ear, arms around my waist, I remembered.

When you want him to pick up speed, you just—

I charged the two men in an unbridled fury, spearing one of them on the other end of the saber. With all of my strength, I threw him over my back for cover—hoping for his sake it killed him.

The horse and I were acting as a single entity. Hellbent on survival, we leaped over a ravine, charging across the smokey field like a misfired flare. A bullet hit the body behind me—once, then twice. Charred trees held remnants of body parts, strewn about from unrelenting explosives. Men called out in agony for their mothers. I gripped the reins tighter, kicked harder. We may as well have been flying, we were galloping so fast, trampling over uncountable fathers, sons and brothers, wiped from the earth under a fallen sky.

The horse snorted as I pulled back, at last locating my division. "You saved my life," I shouted, slipping down from my mount. "Now I'll save yours—go!" My companion hesitated. *"Go!"* I shouted angrily, slapping him on the rear. "Get out of here!"

I grabbed my shotgun from the back and booked it toward my men.

"Captain!" Thelander yelled. I thought I saw a glint of a smile on the face of the young sergeant when he spotted me. "Captain, I—"

The earth erupted like a volcano, sending dirt flying in every direction. Death would've been more merciful.

I fell to Thelander's side. "It's nothing—it's nothing at all," I reassured, caressing his face with one hand, while pressing the opposite on his stomach, trying desperately to keep everything in.

His lips parted, eyes inching downward.

"Victor—don't look at that, look at me."

"Thompson!"

"You're going to be fine," I promised, sputtering like a broken record. "You're going to be okay, Thelander."

"Thompson—stop shaking him!"

"They'll fix you up just fine—they will."

"HOLDEN!"

A friendly hand gripped my shoulder, and snapping from my trance, I released the dead kid staring back at me with blue lips.

"He's gone," Beckham shouted.

Bewildered, I stared into the burning smog. It was *Revelations*. Complete annihilation. This was the end of the world, and no one would ever believe we'd seen it.

By the time the canal was taken successfully, nineteen hours had passed, and evening rain clouds had slipped over the battlefield, smothering the light of the stars. Puddles formed around the bodies, supplying the water for tomorrow's wildflowers as we trudged through the sludge, scouting for wounded.

Leaving Beckham and Spofford behind, I headed over to check the wood line, swinging a lantern at my side as I scanned the ground for any sign of life. A cigarette hung limply from my bottom lip, too damp to keep a light. I had just reached the edge of the battlefield when I heard a low, nasally sigh.

I squinted at the darkened tree line through the rain, raising the glowing lantern to eye level. "Hello?"

The wounded horse kept trying to stand—only to slip and fall back in the mud. Then, consumed with madness, he would try again. And again. My lips trembled, stinging with muted profanity. I couldn't watch it anymore.

"No," I shouted, running over to him. "Stop!"

I knelt at his side, holding him in place with my palm. There were three visible bullet holes in the abdomen, rising up and down with each panicked breath. Raindrops rolled off his smokey coat, revealing untainted pearl beneath.

"I told you to get out of here," I murmured weakly, knowing damn well there was nowhere for him to go.

As if he recognized my voice, the large eye looked up at me.

"Someone I…" I hung my head. My tears were warm like the rain as they fell down my cheeks with little resistance. "She loves horses." Gently stroking his wet, tangled mane, I pulled my pistol from its holster. "I'm sorry for this," I whispered, cocking the trigger. My voice shook, but my hand was steady. "I'm sorry we did this."

Only the symphony of beating droplets spoke back to me. That shot was the loudest one.

The casualties of man's Armageddon—its dead innocents and singed landscapes—were enough to sour even the most adamant patriot. By the following morning, we were incinerated shells of ourselves. We were barely human.

"I'm sorry, Spof." I reached for my forehead, wiping the sweat from my brow. "What did you say?"

Rick crossed his arms over his chest, bumping my shoulder as we walked. "I said the boys found another one."

"Ah."

"What do you want to do with him?"

"Take him to the others."

"You don't want to talk to him?"

We came to a standstill. The tunnel bustled with Aussies and Americans shuffling in and out. Beckham stood at its edge as two sergeants dragged the German POW out and into the morning sun.

"What's his rank?" I asked.

"Major."

I nodded slowly to myself, biting the inside of my lip. "Actually—bring him here," I said, reaching for my cigarettes.

"Bring him here!"

I struck a match, glaring ahead as the two sergeants brought the prisoner over with Beckham trailing behind. The captured man looked about thirty, if not a little older. He was thin and measly—educated, likely wealthy, cowardly—the kind of officer who hid behind his status, who'd send rows of younger men to die without a second thought.

"At ease," I said, nodding to the pair of sergeants. "We can take it from here."

They released his arms and turned back to the tunnel, leaving us. I looked the major up and down, gripping the cigarette between my fingers with enough tension to snap it in half.

"Schöner Morgen, nicht wahr?" I asked.

It was clear to him that I was being factitious as we both stood there, covered in yesterday's blood. A beautiful morning indeed.

"It is for me, anyway," I added, flicking my ash to the ground. He lifted his eyes, and I smiled at him, swallowing the bile that wanted to creep up my throat. "Cat got your tongue?"

"My English…nicht gut," he said.

"I'll be doing most of the talking."

Rick spit to the ground, exchanging a quick glance with Beckham.

I raised my fingers to my chin, cocking my head to the left. "Geh und stell dich zu diesem Baum."

Doing as I said, the German stepped past me, making his way to the nearest tree.

Rick tugged my sleeve. "What are you doing?"

"Relax. I'm just having a bit of fun." I yanked my arm back. "Go on," I ordered, turning my attention back to the scene at hand.

The prisoner slowed his step, almost as if he could feel me pulling the knife from my belt. He turned over his shoulder, meeting my eye with bated breath as it sliced through the air, past his head and into the charred tree in front of him.

"Sorry. Wurden sie bitte?" I asked, motioning to the knife sticking out of the trunk.

Obediently, he faced forward and reached for it as I slipped the second from my belt.

"Come on, Thom," Beckham squeaked from behind. "This isn't fun—"

The German moved his hand just in time to avoid the second knife.

"Ah! By the skin of your teeth, Major," I called out. "But eventually, one's luck runs out!" I started the walk to retrieve my knives.

"Sie lesen gerne!" the German shouted suddenly, pointing to my chest. Caught off guard, I looked to the book that was partially sticking out of my pocket. "Sie lesen gerne!"

I furrowed my brow, annoyed.

He motioned a finger to me, then reached into his pants pocket, pulling out a book of his own. "Ich auch. Ich unterrichte Schreiben!" he exclaimed, pointing to the book. "Ich bin Lehrerin!"

My heart skipped, sending panic signals racing through my chest. My mind slipped backward to another time. Another me. His lips moved, but I didn't hear the words. I didn't care what they were.

"WHOA!" Rick shouted, redirecting my pistol's barrel to the ground with his palm.

"Bitte! Bitte!" begged the man. "Ich bin Lehrerin, ich—"

"What's he saying?"

"Shut up," I threatened, snatching him by the collar. "Shut up! Or I will put a bullet in your fucking head!"

He begged. He pleaded. He listed reasons left and right on why I shouldn't kill him.

"Goddamnit, I said *shut up!*" I yelled, pressing the barrel to his forehead.

"What are you doing?!"

I could tell by the tone of Beckham's voice he was horrified, but I was as deaf to reason as the God the German petitioned under his breath.

"On your knees, then. If you're going to pray," I said, shoving him to the ground.

I wiped my forehead, trembling with adrenaline as he kneeled before me, already paler than a corpse.

"Enough!" Rick shoved himself between us, hand up in protest. "Not like this."

"Out of the way. Out of the way or so help me—"

"Or you'll shoot me, Holden?"

"Stop trying to be a hero," I warned. "I'll kill him at your feet, Rick—I don't care."

"Because the world's on fire anyway? Another body won't make a damn bit of difference!"

"Move," I commanded, clutching the gun tighter. "That's an order, Lieutenant."

Begrudgingly, he obeyed—but not without murmuring over his shoulder as he walked past me. "This isn't who you are."

He was wrong. He didn't know who I was. He didn't know how my soul had been spliced.

I gritted my teeth, focusing in on the beads of sweat that dripped from the man's forehead. His brow wrinkled in anticipation as he stared at the ground, breathing shallowly his last breaths. One bullet to settle the score. For them. For me. The sweet notion of retribution laid in my hands, yet the weight of my finger on the trigger felt like unmovable lead.

I looked to the sky, dropping my arm.

"Danke! Danke! Ich—"

"God damn you!"

A hard smack across the face with my pistol left him unconscious. I reached for the novel in my pocket, chucking it to the ground next to him. The photo of the child, which had halfway fallen out, peered up at me from the edge. "A life for a life," I murmured bitterly.

I walked past my lieutenants without another word, tossing the gun in the grass between them.

"Answer me this, Thom," Rick said at last as we sat together above the quarry.

"Okay."

"That German. What'd he say to you?"

"That he was a writing teacher." Dropping my voice, I picked at the bandage on my hand. "He saw the book in my pocket."

His stare was the noisiest kind—full of questions, and if I'd known that it would be his last night alive, I might have answered them.

"You're a better man than me, Spof," I admitted, looking at the red stinger planet, flickering above.

Arm resting on his knee, Rick eyed me with a quiet stoicism. "That's just another story you've been telling yourself."

"Hey, fellas."

We whipped around to see Beckham standing behind us.

"I know we're heading out to clear those tunnels tomorrow, it's just that…uh, there's something wrong with my typewriter, and I'd really like to write Dora beforehand. You don't figure you could maybe…"

"Sure, Beck." I perked up with a grin, though it was too dark for him to see it. "I can take a look at it."

A Midnight Train
Paris, January 22, 1919

I readjusted myself on the flimsy mattress, stirred to consciousness by a door slamming upstairs. Beside me, a third of a bottle of wine that I'd picked up on my walk home from the church and the scattered papers of my short story. In my hand, a pencil.

It was dark out. By the look of the sky, I was sure it was well into the morning hours when I flipped my wrist over to check the time.

10:22 p.m.

Groggy, and still a little drunk, I rubbed my eye with the back of my hand and reached for one of the papers, tossing it in the air. I stood up, peeking around the corner into Dane's empty bedroom.

Silence.

"Hm. Wonder where he got off to."

Lady hopped up onto the window's ledge, and I followed her, grabbing the wine bottle from the floor.

A middle-aged couple walked arm in arm beneath the dim lit windows of the 5th arrondissement, looking smitten as a pair of doves. Diverting my eyes, I reached for my pack of cigarettes in my shirt pocket. *"What?"* I asked, feeling Lady's stare.

She only blinked her sleepy eyes and tapped her tail, signaling that I should very well know.

"Of course, I miss her." I sighed hopelessly, watching the couple through the reflection of my match. "But it's better this way."

The kitten, omniscient in her Egyptian wisdom, narrowed her gaze on me.

"She doesn't need my baggage."

Lady turned back to the window, flicking her tail condescendingly.

"Besides" —I did the same, again finding the couple as I sipped from the wine bottle— "she's probably found someone else by now."

Surely, she had. I could picture the line of suitors at her front door, jumping for the opportunity to take her out while I complained to my cat. I glanced at the mattress on the floor, cold and barren, and I thought of how she'd fit perfectly against me as we slept. With a faint smile, I allowed the warm recollection to permeate my skin like the sun after a long day by the riverside. Lady brushed up against my hand with a sweet purr.

"I know what you *really* want." I walked into the kitchen. Grabbing the nearest can of tinned meat, I popped it open with my knife, cutting around the top. "Here you go," I said, scooting it over to her.

When I turned back to the street, the couple had vanished, as if they were a trick of my brain, created only to taunt me. I imagined them squeezing into a cab together with his arm around her shoulder, with plans to wake up next to each other and drink coffee in the morning—the envy of the rest of us who'd chosen to be lonely.

I exhaled, grabbing the wine from the windowsill. "Do you think she misses me?"

Lady glanced up from the can, licking her lips.

I shot back the bottle, gulping the last few sips. "I hope you're right."

. . .

The household was asleep—this much was clear, but Camille's room, just left of center, was still lit as the cab pulled up outside of her gate. I glanced down at my watch.

11:46 p.m.

Careful not to wake anyone, I shut the door quietly behind me. I walked down the side alley, where barren trellises climbed up the wall to the empty garden boxes outside of each window. Just under the glow of her bedroom, I imagined her lying in a sheaf nightgown, like a muse of a romance painter, drifting in and out of dreams. But they wouldn't be my dreams. Not tonight.

I reached down and picked up a pebble, launching it at her window. Then another. About a minute later, she came to the window and unlatched it, looking out into the mysterious night.

"Down here."

"Holden!" she gasped.

I peered up at her with a giddy smile.

"What are you doing here?"

"I've got a midnight train to catch," I whispered. "I'm hoping I'm not too late."

"What?"

I tried again, raising my voice. "I said, I—"

"Shhh." She laid her finger gracefully over her lips. "You're going to wake my father."

"Okay." I shrugged. "Just a minute, then."

"Holden, no! What are you—"

Leveraging myself up onto the nearest trellis, I grabbed onto one of the Georgian-style ledges of the brick house, pulling myself up to her second-storey window.

"You're crazy!" She leaned over me. "You're going to break your leg!"

Happy to see her, I couldn't stop smiling. "Worth it," I whispered, kissing her cheek. "I've missed you."

"You've been drinking." A look of reservation washed over her. "She said you would do this exact thing."

"Who said I would do what?"

"I saw Marge the other day," she said, leaning against the window's edge. "She told me that Jeanne, her new housekeeper, overheard her talking about our night out at the cinema."

I could've swallowed my fucking tongue.

"It seems she knows you quite well."

"She really doesn't…"

"She told Marge that you'd disappear for a while, then show back up when you were bored enough."

"I'm sorry for the silence. I just get…"

"'He'll bat his baby blues at her—say he's sorry, just long enough to get what he wants.'"

I gripped the window. "Camille, that's not what this is."

"She said you'd say that, too."

"Of course she would!" Loud enough to attract the attention of a late-night walker who halted outside the alley, I pressed myself against the building, lowering my voice back to a whisper. "Of course, she'd say that—she's jealous! She wants me miserable!"

"Understandably so. She told Marge that she'd been with you only a few months ago."

"Camille…"

"And can you believe I told my cousin she had to be mistaken?" She laughed sharply. "Denial is such a pretty thing."

"It was only twice. Once the night we met, and then another time shortly after. It was before—"

"Twice too many," she snapped.

"It was before I really knew you!"

"Why are you playing with me?"

"Camille! I'm no—would you just listen to me?"

"I'd already let go of you! I'd done my grieving."

Still clutching onto the window, I stammered, "You'd already let go of me? It was that easy for you?"

"I was well on my way until you climbed up from the grave."

I swallowed hard, catching a glimpse of the gown peeking beneath her silk robe. "Were you out with someone else tonight?" I didn't give her a chance to answer. "Let me guess," I said, grabbing onto the shutter and hoisting myself up to eye level with her. "That sorry sap you stood up, right?"

"He may be sorry but at least he's not amoral," she replied, stepping back as I seated myself on her windowsill.

"If you go out with him again then it's you who's playing with me," I countered.

"Surely you don't think I'm going to sit around and cry over you."

"I'm here, aren't I? Doesn't that mean anything?" I licked my lips, then looked up at her. "My actions haven't been ideal, I know —but I came here hoping you'd give me a chance to explain."

Camille crossed her arms, stepping closer. "Why should I?"

"Because I think you know the night we spent together was different than any night I ever spent with Jeanne."

Her shoulders loosened, and she unclenched her jaw, dropping her arms to both sides.

"Or anyone for that matter," I added.

"You put on a good act."

"I'm not acting," I said, reaching for her hand.

She didn't fight me when I pulled her in, taking her face in my hands. The instant our lips touched, I knew she'd missed me, too. "I know what I have now, and I'll be better," I assured, pecking her nose as we parted. "I promise you that."

"You don't have it anymore."

My eyes shot up starkly at her response, questioning if I'd heard her correctly. "What?" I squeaked stupidly.

"*I said* you don't have it anymore."

I stared blankly.

"The damage is done..."

"But you kissed me back."

Her tone was sad and far away. "I'm sorry."

"No." I laughed, turning away. "I'm the one who's sorry—

sorry for coming here. Have fun with what's-his-name." I lowered myself down from the window ledge, stepping foot on the trellis, then the ground.

"Holden—wait! Please don't be so angry with me!"

Shoving my hands in my pockets, I hustled back toward the street, forcing my vision forward as if looking back would turn me to a salt pillar.

Intrusive thoughts of her faceless new beau flooded my mind as I passed by the neighboring mansions, dripping with French aristocracy. He probably owned one of them, complete with a window-lit kitchen for her baking. He would be able to give her everything she'd ever wanted, and she'd settle for a lackluster man who was fine with second place. Cut from the same cloth, her parents would gush over him to their friends and my name would become a forgotten relic of her youth, a dusty book pulled from the shelf only on her loneliest nights.

I kicked a pebble with my shoe. Whoever he was, I fucking hated him.

A car door shut, distracting me momentarily from my self-imposed hell. Under the streetlights, a porcelain wrist extended from the cab, grabbing hold of her date's hand. She stepped out, adjusting her hat as the man turned around to see me gaping at them from the curb.

"Bonsoir," he said, acknowledging me.

I forced a polite grin as I passed by the couple I'd watched from the window of our flat.

From behind the safety of her front door, Vanina's eyes grew wide. She'd answered the precarious knock about an hour and a half later—the time it had taken me to catch a cab to Montmartre, then walk to her flat in the numbing cold. "What are you doing here?" she asked. "It's late."

I stood before her like a stray dog. "I went by *Le Royal* but you weren't there. Can we talk?"

She pursed her lips sourly, as if to remind me that I hadn't answered her question.

"It's kind of a long story."

"I thought you wanted to talk," she prodded.

I lifted both shoulders, then dropped them in a pitiful shrug. "The girl I was seeing…she just broke it off."

She looked past my shoulder and onto the muted street. "You're seeing someone."

"I *was*," I corrected.

"You came here to tell me that?"

"Maybe," I admitted. "I guess I…"

She waited, arms crossed.

"I just didn't want to be alone."

My eyes scanned the room of the shabby duplex as I followed her inside—from the scattered dolls across the floor to the sewing machine under the window, then to the musty lamp in the corner.

"Emma is asleep," she said. "Would you like any tea? It's still warm from earlier."

"Yes. Thank you," I replied, inspecting the sewing machine.

"I'd offer you sugar, but…"

A familiar token on her end table seized my attention, and I circled around for a better look. Embroidered postcard in hand, I turned around to see her staring at me. "Black is fine," I assured.

Nodding, she walked over and handed me a teacup.

"You kept it," I said, returning the card back to the picture frame it was propped against.

Vanina took a seat on the sofa, and I joined her, resting the teacup on my thigh.

"How are…things?" I asked, warming my fingers.

"Fine." She raised her cup, taking a sip so small it had to be for show. "I'm sorry if I've missed you. I had to cut back hours."

"You haven't. I've been a little preoccupied lately."

"Miss Helene came down with a winter cold, so she's been unable to watch Emma."

"Are you glad?"

She looked down, rotating her teacup on the saucer. "Money is important," she replied. "It's the most important thing, when you're alone."

I dropped my voice low—so low I wasn't even sure if she heard me. "Of course."

"And you?" she asked, snapping herself from whatever grim thought she'd been lost in. "Aside from what brought you here."

"Never better," I lied, clumsily setting my cup back on the saucer while trying to balance it on my leg. "I'm great."

We exchanged smiles in mutual agreement that neither of us were in the mood for honesty.

I looked down at her half empty teacup on the table's edge. "You've hardly touched your tea."

"I was heading to bed when you knocked."

I raised my brows, spinning the empty teacup on its plate before setting it on the table next to hers. "Do you think I'm *amoral?*" I asked, glancing up to meet her.

She stood up—a clear sign she was ready to retire. "I don't know you well enough to say," she replied, grabbing a blanket and laying it across the top of the couch for me.

I laid down, bringing the quilt to my chin before turning over my shoulder to look at her. "Thank you," I said, patting the sofa's top.

She reached for my hand, squeezing it weakly. "Goodnight," she said, pulling the string of the lamp.

I listened to the sound of her footsteps fade around the corner and her bedroom door creak open, but not close behind her. Facing front on the couch, I shifted my attention to the silk postcard sitting on the end table. I'd been around enough to know what a cracked bedroom door really meant, but for formality's sake, I waited ten minutes.

I ran my finger across the plaster wall in a quiet confidence as I approached Vanina's door and pushed it open, halting in the doorway to be sure.

She stared back at me from her place in bed. "This is why you're here, isn't it?" she asked softly.

I shut the door, engulfing us in a sensual anonymity. Her fingers dug into my arms when I reached her, guiding me under the covers. She pulled my shirt off as I spread her legs with my knee, pressing my mouth to hers in a misplaced, recoiled, powder keg of a kiss. My imagination ran wild in the privacy of the dark, muddled with fervid visions of mousy waves caught between my fingers and hazel eyes looking back at me. I wanted her desperately. In my bed—in the morning light, covered with flour in the kitchen. I envisioned it was *her* jawline I was kissing, her breath in my ear. I could almost make myself believe it.

Vanina slowed, likely feeling the disconnect.

"I'm sorry," I whispered.

"You miss her."

I rolled over on my back, rubbing my face with both hands.

"It's okay," she added. "I was thinking of someone else, too."

"You were?"

Vanina curled up next to me without a word, and I brought her cheek to my chest.

"Emma's father?" I asked. "Is that who you were thinking about?"

"You remind me of him," she admitted. "They never met. He was a soldier—like you. With dark hair like yours."

"Where is he now?"

Her silence was answer enough.

"I'm sorry," I whispered. Despite grief being a faithful friend of mine, I could think of nothing better to say.

"I met him when my town was under occupation."

"He was German?"

She went on. "Neither of us understood the other's language, but we could both speak English. No one ever knew what we were saying to each other."

"But eventually his orders came," I added, knowing all too well what that was like. "Did he know about her? About Emma."

"He died at Verdun without ever receiving my letter." Vanina paused. She hadn't forgotten that I was in the AEF, that her lover was my enemy, and I was trained to hate him. "You disapprove."

"No." I shook my head, brushing the fine blonde hair from her cheek. "*Ich leibe dich*," I whispered.

Her sigh was soft and melancholic, like she'd just woken up from a dream only to realize she was lying against me and not him.

"When I was stationed in Belgium, I met somebody, too," I said.

"What happened?"

"Her farm was shelled, all but the house. An old Flemish man answered the door when I came knocking…I couldn't understand what he was saying, but he was able to point me to her grave by the barn." I paused, suddenly aware of the knot in my throat. "I don't even know if she suffered."

"Was she your last lover before this recent one?"

I let out a hesitant laugh.

"I see," she replied. "You've had many."

"Too many," I admitted. "It's a habit I can't seem to shake. It's what got me into this mess."

I could feel her eyes studying me, inquisitive and curious. "Why do it then? Give yourself to so many if you don't have to."

"I don't know."

Vanina shuffled a bit in my arms. "Then perhaps you *are* amoral."

"I suppose it just" —I turned my cheek to face her— "makes me feel like I'm in control."

"The same reason I brought you to my bed tonight. It's nice to pretend." She sat up abruptly, glancing over her shoulder to look at me. "But you never tried to touch me, all the times you could have." Her words lingered in the dark. "I would've let you."

"Because I could never be certain it was consensual," I said quietly. "I wouldn't have wanted you to feel like I was holding something over you."

Vanina was quiet for a long while. "If I didn't know any better, I'd…" The softness of her voice rattled my bones. "If it's not too presumptuous to say—"

I could feel my cheeks turning hot. "It's not."

A long pause followed as she searched for my hand in the dark. "Then I'd say you know what that feels like," she said, finding it.

My Last Revision
Princeton, September 1916

I peered at Holder tower from the edge of campus—standing like a watchful lighthouse on an angry sea—before wiping my palms across my pants and turning over my shoulder once more, relieved to see an empty street behind me.

I'd hardly heard him when I'd blasted through the screen door of the cottage, stumbling into broad daylight with my pants still undone.

"Holden—you're being a little dramatic, don't you think?"

I squeezed my eyes shut, trying to shake off his words that still stuck to my skin.

"Fix yourself at least, will you?"

I leaned back on the nearest tree and unfastened my belt, noting a group of football players wrapping up their morning practice. Readjusting it to its proper loop, I watched with envy as they scattered leisurely across the lawn into their cliques. The rest of the courtyard—littered with Princetonians lounging in the grass as squirrels watched curiously from the sidelines—was just as I'd left it a few hours prior. For them, it was just another day.

"INCOMING!!"

I turned to see a football flying at my head and Theo on its tail. I ducked.

"Nice catch," he called, watching it land next to me.

I stared at the ball on the ground as he and Scott sprinted over.

"Off your game this morning, Thompson," Scott teased. "Long night?"

I crossed my arms over my chest. My heart palpitated nervously beneath, as if they might somehow be able to *tell*. "Just tired. I worked on my story all night," I replied.

"Such a teacher's pet—always working off the clock." Theo laughed, shooting Scott a look. "How'd critique day go?"

I dropped my eyes to the ground. My story. I'd been so proud of it when I set out that morning. "Oh, you know."

"Can I read it?"

"What about your story? You're just going to leave it?"

"I left it at Frank's," I said.

"Well," said Theo, catching Scott's pass, "when you get it back, I'd love to read it."

In my mind, I summoned the street view from his living room window. The neighbor walking his dog. The wren that had watched from his place on the branch, just beyond my reach. I wouldn't be getting it back.

"I'm only kidding about the teacher's pet thing," Theo added. "Not everyone is lucky enough to have an established author take them under their wing."

"What?" I asked, snapping back to attention.

"I'm only saying I get it." He threw the ball back to Scott. "It's all about who you know."

Looking past them, I spotted a few members of the Triangle Club, meeting over a picnic table lunch. Theo was right. I was no different than any of the other aspiring writers who'd walked into his class that day. What was it about *me*?

FALL 1914——————

Trailing behind an ensemble of confused whispers, I'd walked quietly through the door, bag slung over my shoulder.

"Where's the professor? There's no one at the desk."

I turned to my classmate. "I don't know," I admitted, searching the empty blackboard for potential clues.

The air smelled like fresh pages of a newspaper, and the room itself was well kept, with bookshelves lining the perimeter. I halted in front of the uninhabited desk. A book lay open across its top, marked up with green ink. Licking my finger, I flipped the page.

"What's that you've got there?"

Tugging the leather strap of my bag, I turned over my shoulder to see someone gripping the edge of a classroom desk, probing me inquisitively.

"In your pocket," he added, motioning to the worn novel sitting comfortably in my sport coat.

The man was all raven hair and dark eyes. I stepped toward him, handing him the book. Lying on his desk was a book turned on its cover, and next to it, a green pen.

"Whitman," he remarked.

I nodded, counting the three gray hairs just above his ear.

"Are you a poet?"

"No," I murmured. "...Sir."

His eyes lit up with enthusiasm. "Well, you caught me," he said. "Nicely done, Mr..."

"Thompson," I replied. "Holden."

"How old are you?"

"Twenty, sir."

"You're old for your class."

"I was saving for tuition."

He couldn't have been more than ten years my senior. Nodding with approval, he handed the book back. "I admire that."

I reached for it, but he gripped tighter.

"You might be wondering why I'm hiding in plain sight."

"To get a proper read of the room?" I guessed.

"I want to see how my students behave when they think no

one's watching," he said, releasing my copy of *Leaves of Grass*. "Tell me, how did you figure me out so quickly?"

"The pen," I replied. "You annotate your books."

"As do you. I'd say that one is well loved."

"My brother gave it to me."

"Did he go to Princeton?"

"No. He's a painter overseas."

"I see." His eyes softened, signaling interest in what I had to say. "And you're sad about that."

"He's my best friend." I shrugged, returning my book to its home in my pocket. "A part of me would like to be there with him."

He groaned. "Careful what you wish for. Europe is a minefield right now."

"Good point." I smiled at him, motioning with my eyes to the title sitting next to his arm. "Who's the author?"

He picked it up, fanning the pages with a grin. "See, this one is mine. I can mark it all I like."

"Your book?" I choked. "You wrote a book?"

"I think I've made them wait long enough, don't you?" He passed his novel off to me and stood up. "Good morning!" he announced, giving rise to a cascade of astonished faces. "Welcome to English. I'm Professor…"

Franklin Lindsay.

I mouthed the name inscribed in gold across the bottom of the leather-bound hardcover.

"To tell you the truth, I've been second guessing it lately," I said, rousing myself to the present.

Theo held onto the ball, staring blankly at me. "What do you mean?"

"Well." I sighed sharply. "The life of a writer is far from glamorous."

"Frank seems to do okay for himself."

"Only because he doesn't have children," I countered. "I wouldn't even have the teacher's salary."

"You think that's why his wife left him?" Theo speculated. "Because he's broke?"

Scott chuckled to himself. "The guys in my eating club say it's because he was a *scoundrel*."

I gulped.

"If anyone knows the reason, it'd be you," he added, shooting me a playful look. "Since you're buddies and all."

Nervously, I bit the hangnail on my index finger. "I don't."

"Check it out." Theo motioned to our left.

We all turned to look as General Heintzelman swept through the courtyard with his downturned smile and widow's peak.

"Looks like he's on a mission."

"He is," said Scott. "Haven't you heard?"

Theo and I shook our heads.

"The university is forming a battalion."

"A battalion?" I asked, turning back to the general, who was talking to one of the students.

"That's right. At least that's what the guys in my eating club said."

"Well then, it's hearsay," Theo protested.

Their voices dissolved into the background as I narrowed my sights on Heintzelman. He stood at attention in his stark, undeniable masculinity. If I'd emitted something similar, maybe I wouldn't be in this position. "Did they say when, Scott?" I asked, rejoining the conversation. "About the battalion."

Theo looked confused, knowing I'd never even so much as held a gun.

"Spring, I think," Scott replied.

I nodded to myself. "Hm. Well, I need to get back."

"That's right," Theo interjected. "It's date night."

Fuck.

"Right—yeah," I stuttered.

Scott grinned like a Cheshire cat. "Is tonight the night?"

"I don't know." I shrugged, pivoting away from them. "I guess we'll see."

I began my walk across the courtyard, feeling as though I could've dreamt the entire conversation. It took everything in me not to run to the arched entryways of Holder Hall—to the safety of its long, ample hallways. I needed to be alone.

Bonnie.

I'd completely forgotten about my plans with Bonnie. I couldn't possibly—but what kind of man would that make me to cancel?

I couldn't cancel.

Ducking into the nearest bush outside of my dormitory, I emptied what little bit was in my stomach. I wiped my mouth, glancing upward at the blinding sun, peeking from behind Holder Tower. A few classmates spoke in hushed whispers as they walked by, probably thinking I was hungover.

Fuck.

I needed to shower.

What I wasn't expecting to find when I swung open the door to my dorm was my roommate, Walter, sprawled across his bed.

"Hey, Holden," he said, glancing over the top of his textbook.

I stared at him, paranoid that I looked as dirty as I felt.

"You okay? Your face is all flushed."

"It's crisper than it looks outside," I replied, backing up against the door to close it. "I thought you had chemistry?"

He tossed his book aside and sat upright. "I'm on my way out."

"Got it," I replied, averting my eyes.

"Are you sure you're all right?"

I paused, hanging my sport coat on the rack. Walter Kincaid—nicest guy I ever knew. I could've guessed he'd ask twice, just to be certain. I nodded reassuringly, turning to him with a grin. "I'm fine."

He exhaled, rising to his feet and swiping a notebook from his bedside table. "Well, hey...do you think you could take a look at my history paper?" He handed it to me. "I could tell you about the Seven Years War from start to finish, but I can't spell worth a shit."

"Sure. I'll look at it."

"Thanks, man."

He didn't seem to notice the way I flinched at the friendly pat of his hand on my shoulder. "No problem, Walter."

"I owe you one," he added on his way out. "Sincerely—I do."

I scanned the familiar trinkets of my home away from home as he locked me in with my thoughts; its wallpapered corners hung with Tiger memorabilia and its mantle littered with textbooks. I shifted my attention to Walter's notebook in my hand, laying it across the desk next to Dane's most recent letter. I skimmed the first couple sentences again. *I'm glad you have someone like Frank to look after you there,* he'd written.

I couldn't look at it.

The empty showers were the sole breadcrumb the universe bestowed upon me that day. I set my towel on the sink, catching a glimpse of myself in the mirror hanging above. My mind raced as I undressed—about Walter's paper, Triangle Club, Bonnie. With each layer of clothing shed, I retreated further into my head, growing more detached from my body, more numb. I didn't dare examine myself. I only wanted to scrub my skin until it bled.

Freezing water rushed from the shower head above, spraying me in a brisk rain. I closed my eyes.

"You'd do well not to make a scene. What would people say?"

I gripped the slippery bridge of my nose, trying to banish the thought. What *would* people say? Dane, Bonnie, my friends—if they knew?

I reached for the soap, scrubbing myself raw, my eyes glossing over with tears. My career as a writer was over before it ever began. All the money I'd saved for tuition, with one measly year of school to go—I'd sold it all for cheap flattery. I'd never forgive myself.

I shut off the faucet and looked at my clothes. They lay innocently in a pile nearby, not knowing they were bound for the incinerator. Grabbing my towel, I dried my face, keeping my eyes on the sink. Someone's forgotten razor sat on its edge. I held the towel to my lips, for the first time considering the scarlet hue of my own blood, and what it might look like spilled over the white porcelain.

I couldn't. Not with Bonnie waiting on me.

I glanced up at the splotchy reflection looking back at me. How blue his irises glowed against the bloodshot sclera. Perhaps if I stared long enough, I might trade places with my double; him out here and myself in the mirror, where I could make myself disappear like a cheap parlor magic trick.

I walked to campus the next morning with Bonnie's scent still on me, an intoxicating cocktail of sweet nectar and sea salt. The first time hadn't quite gone the way I'd imagined. Overly eager, I'd plowed ahead too fast, ultimately ending our tryst prematurely. The second time was much better—*I* was much better. Supplied with newfound confidence, I skipped my first class and headed straight to the transfer office. And when they asked what course of study I wanted to change to, I picked the last place anyone would look for me.

"Thompson—wait up!"

I was walking after class when I heard Theo call my name from across the courtyard. I slowed, allowing him to catch up.

"What's going on?" he demanded.

"What do you mean?"

"Cut the bullshit—you know exactly what I mean."

I turned to him combatively.

"Walter told me you enrolled in Military Tactics this morning," he added, out of breath from chasing me down. "That's a hell of a decision to make before noon."

"Sorry, am I guilty of something?"

"Giving up on your dream, for one! And after everything you've said about your brother in Italy?"

"Things change."

"You're the most talented guy I know." He let out an irritated sigh. "You love writing more than anything. Why the revision?"

I bit my tongue, looking to the autumn leaves overhead.

"I'm your friend," he pressed.

"It's just not sustainable Theo," I said finally. "I want a wife and a family and house. Dreams change."

"...wait a minute."

Every muscle in my body clenched.

"Are you in love with Bonnie?"

I relaxed, relieved by the conclusion he'd drawn.

"I knew it! I knew *something* had happened."

I forced a smile, dropping my eyes to the ground.

"You can't blame me for being curious." Theo paused, his eyes narrowing on something behind me. "And looks like I'm not the only one."

I glanced over my shoulder to see Frank standing on the edge of the cloister. The blood running through my veins turned to ice.

"He's got the look of someone who just lost his star pupil," Theo joked as I turned back to face him. "Well, I guess that's my cue. See you later?"

I wanted to grab him by his coat and beg him not to leave my side—help me avoid the inevitable confrontation—but I couldn't bring myself to do it. "See you later," I said.

I watched Theo walk away, but my focus was on the crunching leaves behind me.

"There you are."

I turned around to see Frank standing behind me, briefcase in hand and suitcases under his eyes.

"I've been looking all over for you."

"What do you want?" I asked.

"I heard you transferred out of my class this morning," he added. "I wanted to make sure you were all right."

That was fucking rich.

"Fine, thanks." I began to walk, hoping he'd take the hint, but his mood was cavalier and personable, like nothing had happened at all.

"You look good! Like a new man. I guess last night went well?"

I lowered my voice, afraid that someone might be listening. "I don't want to talk about this with you."

"Of course not," he said, crossing in front of me. "I didn't come here for that."

Diverting my eyes to the ground, I smiled, imagining all the ways I'd like to see him dead.

"Five minutes of your time," he pleaded, raising his hands. "I just want to talk."

Maybe it was because he was technically my superior—or maybe, in some warped way, I still craved his approval. I can't tell you why I agreed, but I did.

Hovering in the doorway of his classroom, I watched as he walked over to his desk and swiped a few loose papers from the top.

"So, Heintzelman's class."

"That's right."

"Are you serious?"

"Dead serious."

He held my eye, dropping the papers into the waste bin next to him. "I guess you won't be needing this anymore, then."

The sight of my story in the trash stung like a hornet. "You're right," I murmured. "I won't."

He sighed, removing his reading glasses. "The whole damn student body is itching to go to war with Germany. But *you*—I didn't take you for much of a patriot."

"Maybe you don't know me as well as you think you do."

He ran his fingers across the corner of the desk, then walked over to me. "I wonder what Dane would think." His nearness made my skin crawl. "Ah," he added with a nod. "You haven't told him yet."

"Maybe I have," I lied.

"Christ, Holden. I don't want to be searching the list of the fallen for your name!"

"Don't pretend you care about what happens to me."

"Don't be ridiculous. You know I do." He looked at me flatly. "What then? You're just going to sacrifice your whole future to get away from me? Is that it?"

"What future?" I countered sharply, stepping back. "Living off campus writing mediocre stories to stay relevant?"

"Now that's a change of tone. Yesterday you were practically begging me to publish you alongside my mediocre stories."

I scoffed. "You're lucky I didn't tell them why I transferred."

"That was probably wise on your part." He laughed to himself, shooting me a knowing look. "If I'm remembering correctly, you didn't exactly shove me away."

"I wanted to."

"Certain context clues would argue otherwise."

If humiliation could kill, it would've struck me down right there, like a merciful bolt of lightning. "I'd just told you about my girlfriend." The words were hot as fire on my lips. "That was hardly an invitation!"

"Keep it down, will you?" Crossing behind me, he shut the door, closing us in. "You think *you're* embarrassed?" he whispered. "What about *me*—I thought…I can't be the only one to blame here when it was you who was unclear."

"*Me?*"

"You wrote me into your story like some kind of muse. What was I supposed to think?"

My mind slipped backward to the suffocating sage-green sitting room—the sound of boiling water overheating and spilling over the sides of the tea kettle. "That's…" My fingers trembled at my side. "You're twisting my words. I said no—"

"If anyone initiated this, it was *you.*"

. . .

THE PREVIOUS MORNING———————

I anxiously watched Frank scan page after page from my seat in the wingback chair. The clock ticked, filling the room with an anticipatory echo as I tried to decipher if his knitted brow was a good or bad omen of the critique to come.

"Well," I huffed nervously, "what do you think?"

He removed his glasses, laying my story on the coffee table. "When you said you had a good one for me last week you weren't bluffing."

"Really?" I perked up. "I was toying around with submitting it to the Princetonian."

He crossed one leg over the other, leaning back on the sofa.

"Oh, out with it," I pressed.

"Not that the Princetonian isn't a great paper, but this has potential for a real publication."

"You really think it's that good?"

"You don't?"

I didn't answer.

"You should have more faith in yourself," he added. "I wish I'd been half as good of a writer at your age."

I looked to the barren hardwood floor. "You're buttering me up."

"I'll tell you what," he said, rising to his feet. He lunged for his desk drawer, digging through its contents. "I've been working on a little side project..."

"What kind of side project?"

He whipped around, meeting my eye gleefully. "A short story anthology."

I gawked at the stack of paper in his arm. Between teaching and the novel he was already commissioned for, I couldn't have imagined he'd have the time for anything else.

"How would you like to be a published author?" he asked.

"You mean..."

"I'd love to include your story."

"Really?" I asked, gripping both arms of the wingback.

"Really. The plot pacing was perfect, dialogue natural...and your protagonist—there was just *something* familiar about him."

I mirrored his grin from my seat in the chair.

"I'm flattered that you wrote me into your story," he added.

"No, I'm the one that's flattered—you're giving me a huge opportunity. It almost doesn't feel right."

He smiled, handing me the papers. "Fancy some tea? I was about to put some on for myself, I can boil more water if you want to stay awhile and talk about it more."

"Definitely. I mean, I need to revise the script I've written for Triangle Club but the play isn't until next month. I don't have any real plans until later."

"Great. I'll be right back," he promised, leaving me in the company of the familiar titles of his bookshelf. I grazed the first few lines of his anthology, feeling its weight in my hands. Me. *A published author.*

"So, what about later?" Frank called from the kitchen.

"What?"

He walked back in, plopping on the sofa in front of me. "You mentioned having plans later."

I passed the anthology back to him. "Oh! I have a date with Bonnie. That's all."

"You've been seeing her for a while now, haven't you?" he asked, setting it neatly next to my story on the coffee table. "Cute little thing."

"Since last spring."

"And how's it working out?"

"It's going well," I replied, rubbing the back of my neck. "At least...I think it is. It's always hard to tell."

"You're preaching to the choir."

I felt a tightness well up in my chest. "Your wife?" I asked timidly.

"That's a conversation for something stronger than tea." He

dropped his eyes, expelling an exasperated sigh. "It's better not to fight it. Just let her carry on thinking I'm as awful as she believes. Easier, anyway."

"I'm sorry," I murmured.

"Enough about that." He turned back to me, resting both arms on the back of the sofa. "Where are you taking your girlfriend to tell her the news?"

"The theater. Then maybe on a walk, or something. Her parents are out of town, so we can stay out as late as we want."

He laughed, clapping both hands together. "Oh, you sly dog. I know what's up your sleeve."

I could feel myself blushing.

"I'll stop my speculating—surely you get enough of that from your friends," he added lightheartedly.

"Believe me, they have their bets going. But Bonnie is a..."

"Prude?"

"Uh—I was going to say Protestant."

"Do you write to her?"

I smiled guiltily.

"A regular troubadour." He chuckled to himself. "I'm sure you won't have any problem convincing her to sleep with you. Hell, I doubt you'll have to do any convincing at all. Not with those bedroom eyes you flash around."

I laughed. "My what?"

"Bedroom eyes. I'm surprised no one's ever pointed them out to you."

"Well...they never worded it like *that*." I cleared my throat and stood up, making my way to browse the bookcase in the corner. The last thing I wanted to divulge was that I'd had exactly zero encounters with a woman in the bedroom. "I don't mind waiting if that's what she wants," I added, pretending to scan the colorful spines.

"Parents out of town..." he mused, standing and following me over. "You might not get another chance like that."

"That's true."

"It's normal to be nervous."

"Who said I was nervous?"

He smiled knowingly, leaning his shoulder up against the bookcase next to me.

"Fuck, is it that obvious?"

"Maybe a little. But you're going to be a published author. Have some confidence."

I smiled weakly.

"You'll see," he added. "When the time comes, it's a piece of cake."

I slid the book I'd picked back in its proper place. "What's the secret, then?" I asked, lowering my voice. "You see, I...don't really have anyone to ask, with Dane being away and all."

He leaned in closer, nodding along.

"I just want to be okay." I turned my cheek to see his hand resting on my shoulder.

"Of course you do."

"I, um." Whatever I'd meant to say, the words dried up as he slid his hand subtly down my chest to my belt. I caught his eye, holding it, but the subtle shake of my head wasn't enough to deter him from unfastening it.

"What're you..."

"The secret is," he began, tugging my belt, "if you want to enchant someone, you have to experience enchantment yourself."

I tried to squeeze past, but he gently pushed my chest with his other hand, keeping me in place against the bookshelf.

"Hold on there. We haven't even talked about the anthology yet," he reminded. "There's a lot of groundwork to cover."

I froze.

He popped open the first button on my pants, then the second.

Feeling a flash of panic, I inhaled shallowly. "I need to go."

"I thought you were interested in a publication."

Just over his shoulder sat my whole future, reduced to a few scattered pieces of paper across a walnut coffee table.

"I am...but..."

There was an unwavering, deliberate hunger in his eyes. "I'm doing you a favor."

"Bu what about the tea?"

I was in deep shit—*God*, I was in deep shit, and without my quicksilver tongue, I may as well have been paralyzed.

Unbuttoning the third button, he reached into my pants. "You're tense."

I squirmed. "Please, don't," I murmured, acutely aware of the betrayal by my own body.

"I've always known you were very special."

I forced my attention to the window. A Carolina wren sat outside, like the ones that guarded the meadow when Dane and I were young.

We would lie beneath the wise old oak—ten and thirteen, respectively—bathing in the evening glow, soaking up the tail end of summer's best. Dane would fall silent against the babbling of the brook, and I'd turn to face him, scuffing my cheek against the flimsy blades of grass. He'd smirk in return, not bothering to open his eyes. We'd make it back in time for supper by a hair, sweaty from racing the last bit of daylight through the fields. And I would be home.

"Hey."

Feeling a delicate pat across my back, I blinked hard, lifting my cheek from the scratchy wool of his shoulder.

"Tea's done."

"*Me?*" I rammed him into the blackboard, smearing whatever he'd written with the back of his coat. "I initiated this?"

"If only your writing had this much passion!"

I crunched his collar in my fists, and he smiled a bit, lowering his voice. "You don't have to pretend with me," he taunted. "We both know you were more than willing."

I reached for my pocketknife.

"Enough, Holden." His pupils followed the blade as I flicked it open. "You've made your point."

"That's what you think," I said, gripping him harder. "How does it feel?"

"Threatening a teacher is more than worthy of expulsion—*let go of me.*"

"Forgive me for not being clear." I lifted the knife to his throat. "I want you to beg," I whispered. "So I can pretend I can't hear you."

"Get out."

"Gladly, *Professor,*" I spat, releasing him.

"You're finished. You'll never be a published author without my help," he choked, holding his throat.

Shaking, I halted halfway between him and the door.

"You're not good enough," he added.

Pocketing my knife, I thrusted the classroom door open, nearly running right into the tall, lanky freshman waiting on the other side. "Is Frank in there?" he asked.

I dropped my eyes to the folder he held in his arms. "Who are you?"

"Jonas. I'm here for a critique."

"Jonas..." I looked him over. *"Jonas Willowby*—I read your piece in the Princetonian. It was really good."

"You're Holden, right?" His bright blue eyes lit up. "You're the editor for Triangle Club. That's a hell of a compliment coming from you!"

I nodded, forcing a smile.

"I wish I could talk more," he said, trying to shuffle past me. "But I'm already—"

I blocked him. "Listen to me, Jonas."

He stepped back, wearing an expression of true bewilderment. "What's the big idea?"

"Get lost," I warned, leading him away from the door. "Turn that corner and don't come back."

THE LUXURY OF CHOICES
PARIS, JANUARY 23, 1919

I PRESSED down on Rick's neck, but it slipped under my bloodied fingers. Even in the low light of the tunnel, I could see his blue eyes fade to gray. I pressed harder, feeling the pulse grow faint.

Thump...thump...thump.

With one cheek squished to the pillow, I reluctantly opened an eye to see Vanina's daughter hovering her finger over my forearm as though she'd been tapping it. I must've been quite a sight to find first thing in the morning—lying across the edge of the bed with my arm dangling off, dead to this world and lost in another.

"Emma," I mumbled, noting the indent in the bed next to me. "Where's your mama?"

"Talking to Mr. Julien."

"Mr. Julien?"

Propping myself up on my elbow, I glanced to the hallway, faintly able to make out the sound of a man's voice. Vanina hadn't mentioned she was expecting anyone that morning—though, to be fair—she hadn't been expecting me either.

"Were you having a dream?"

I turned to Emma, scooping my shirt from the floor. "I was."

"What was it about?"

My eyes snapped back to the bedroom door. "Just an old friend," I replied, standing up and walking past her.

Peering down the hall, I could see Vanina standing in the kitchen in her nightgown. Blocking the front door, was a balding man, about forty, fresh off the pipe. On his wrist, a silver chain.

"I see that you're paid, taken care of—you *and* the girl," he snapped, dabbing the edge of his sweat-soaked collar.

"And I'm grateful for everything you've done for us," Vanina replied.

"Are you?" Tempering his voice, he laid his hands over her shoulders. "All I'm asking for is a few more hours—a few extra hours of work from my best girl."

I grimaced sourly, concealed from their line of sight.

"There's no reason you can't bring her in and have the other girls watch her," he went on.

"I couldn't possibly do that."

"Do you have any idea how much money I've lost this week?"

"Ow—you're hurting me."

"How many of our beloved customers have come by looking for you?"

I grabbed Emma's shoulder as she tried slip past my legs. "No, no. Up we go—" I whispered, lifting her. "I want you to stay right here until Mr. Julien leaves," I said, setting her on the edge of the bed. "Can you do that for me?"

She nodded obediently.

"Good girl."

I slipped quietly into the hall, wiping the reassuring grin from my face.

"My soft spot for you has come back to bite me," said the man, brushing the back of his knuckles across Vanina's cheek. "Now I can see that I've spoiled you."

"You're high," she spat, turning away.

Her eyes found mine as I stood in the hallway. I lifted my brows, as if to suggest intervening, but she shot me down with a cutting glance.

"You think you've got me wrapped around your finger," he said, cornering her. "Don't you?" Vanina stumbled backward into the kitchen table. Snatching a handful of her hair, he forced her over it. "Well, I'll teach *you* to forget who's in charge!"

He'd hardly slipped her nightgown up before I had him pinned to the wall with my forearm across his neck.

"Who the hell are you?" he demanded, squirming against my iron hold.

"Holden! Stop!"

"Collecting strays again, Vanina?"

"Don't look at her—you and I are talking now. Look at *me.*" I lowered my voice to a near whisper, tracing his face with a gentle, icy regard. "If you ever so much as come near this address," I threatened, "I will fucking kill you. Do you understand me?"

"You're just another—"

"I will strangle you with my bare hands, and I'll be glad to do it." I let go, grabbing his shirt as he collapsed into a heap of coughing.

"You're a fool," he uttered.

"I'll see you out," I added, shoving him out the door and into the daylight.

"You'll see," he taunted, holding his neck as he stumbled into the street. "You'll see what she's made of sooner or—"

Slamming the door, I turned around to see Vanina leaning against the back of the sofa. She stared down at the splintered, wood floor planks.

"Did he hurt you?"

"I don't need another man to come and save me," she snapped. "I had it under control."

"It didn't look like it," I argued. "At least not from where I was standing."

"He wasn't going to do anything!"

"Vanina! *Listen to what you're saying.*"

"It's not like it is with the other girls." Shaking frantically, she reached up to touch her temple. "He's given me extra money when I needed it for Emma, and—" Seemingly struck by the sight of her own blood, she froze in place.

"Abusers bank on selling empty promises," I said, moving her hair away from the cut to examine it. "Never believe for a single second that he wouldn't sell your soul on a dime."

"Easy for you to say, Holden," she retorted, her eyes blank with disenchantment. "You've had the luxury of choices." The color drained from her cheeks, leaving behind an opalescent hue. I caught her in my arms before she hit the floor. "I'm fine," she stammered, warily clutching onto me.

Gently, I brought my arm beneath her knees and scooped her up. Holding her limp body against me, I pushed the bathroom door open with my shoulder and looked around. It was a drab scene, with broken tile and a film covering the porcelain fixtures, but it would do. I set her down, kneeling next to the tub. "You're all worked up," I said, reaching for the faucet.

Vanina rubbed her eyes, leaning against the sink as I checked the temperature of the water.

"There you are," I said, turning back to her.

"But I—"

"I'll take care of her."

Her eyes darted to the filling tub, then to me.

"Just let me help you," I pleaded softly. "You can trust me."

Cradling a doll in her lap, Emma sat on the living room floor, eyeing me curiously as I closed the bathroom door behind me.

I looked to the three potatoes resting on the kitchen windowsill. "Want to see me do a trick?"

Emma nodded.

I walked over and plucked a potato from the pile, tossing it in the air. "Watch—I'll turn these into something edible," I said, catching it.

About an hour later, I found myself outside the bathroom. Vanina hadn't made a peep since I'd left her.

"It's unlocked," she said, as if she could sense my knuckle hovering over the door. "Come in."

I cracked it open.

Vanina's right arm dangled over the edge of the clawfoot tub, her cheek resting daintily on top. "Where is she?"

"Asleep on the sofa," I replied, squaring my shoulders. "Are you feeling better?"

"I am."

"Glad to hear it." Taking a step back, I nodded to her politely, taking my leave.

"Sit with me," she said, extending her arm.

I hesitated, but only for a moment.

Covering herself in the tub, she watched as I crossed the distance between us, sliding my back down the wall until I was parallel to her on the floor. Chin resting on the tub's edge, she looked me over intently as I settled in beside her. "You're good with her," she said. "I could hear you in the kitchen."

I smirked, thinking of how Emma had sat at the table, listening to me go on about the faraway land of Ireland—the greenest place in the world where nothing grew but potatoes—as she watched me peel the skins in long spirals.

"Do you have any children?"

"Just a younger sister back home," I said, reaching into my pocket. Vanina's mouth curled into a faint smile as I unveiled a silver dollar potato cake wrapped within the linen cloth. I broke off a piece and held it to her lips. "I thought you might be hungry, too."

She took the bite from my fingers, raising her hand to catch any stray crumbs.

I lifted a knee and rested my arm on it, glancing over at her as I broke off another piece. "I grew up eating these. My mother would make them all the time when we were young."

"Why haven't you gone back home to your family?"

I shifted on the floor, bringing my other knee up. "Because it doesn't feel like home anymore. Nowhere does."

She turned away with a subtle nod, as if she were afraid I might hear her thoughts. Questions of where she'd go and what she'd do—how she'd feed her daughter. I admired the worry lines on otherwise youthful skin as she stared ahead with bewitching beauty.

"Hear me out," I said suddenly. "What if the reason things aren't working for us here is because we're supposed to be somewhere else?"

Her lips parted in question as she turned back to me.

"We could leave this place. You, me and Emma."

"Leave Paris?" She plunged herself into the bath, and I followed, peeking over the edge of the tub to find her looking up at me from the cloudy water, green with reluctance.

"I'm serious," I added.

"I know you are."

I gripped the porcelain edge, leaning over. "What do you say?"

She sat up, covering her breasts with one arm. "You're so young," she said, reaching for my face.

I brought my hand to hers as it rested on my cheek, transferring my warmth to her. "Only as young as I feel."

"We hardly know each other."

"I've told you things I've never told anybody."

She sighed, drawing her hand away.

"We could start fresh," I added. "Be in a whole new place by tomorrow evening."

"What a thought." She inched closer, just enough to wet the hair on my arm. Up until that point, I'd been in control of myself, and my thoughts of how obviously naked she was. But now, her skin was glistening and covered in goosebumps, the ends of her hair were dripping with water, and I was feeling a lot of things.

"There's a little village just north of here called Corbie," I went on. "Seated right along a canal. I spent some time there."

"What about her? Camille."

"It's over." I shook my head. "It does me no good to think about it anymore."

A long pause followed, and I held my breath, watching as she dropped her eyes to our touching skin, and then lifted them back to me. She wanted me to make a move. *I was sure of it*—and then she spoke.

"Tomorrow, then?"

"Tomorrow," I whispered, reaching across the tub's rim and kissing her lips.

She pulled me into her, soaking my shirt. I opened my eyes in a hazy pleasure, wetting my bottom lip and then brushing it against hers, but she drew away, searching my gaze attentively.

I didn't stop her when she grabbed my belt, pecking me on the corner of my mouth, then bringing her cheek to mine. Not even as she reached into my pants. The water splashed over the rim as I leaned further over, catching her damp, tangled hair in my fingers. It was fastly apparent that Vanina was skilled in the art of helping men forget their troubles, their wives, their heartbreak.

"Don't stop," I pleaded quietly.

Sensing I was on the precipice, she gripped tighter, and I kissed her eagerly, clutching the edge of the bathtub in relief. Throbbing with rapture on the comedown, I moved her hand away, unable to handle the sensitivity of her touch.

"Let's go now," she said, submerging her fingers into the bath water, shaking off its droplets. "To Corbie."

"Now?" I'd hardly recovered, no less processed what just happened. "I have to talk to my brother first," I added, struggling to readjust my pants. "I can't just disappear without a trace. I can't do that to him."

She grabbed both of my hands, running her fingers over the raised veins. There was sadness to the way she held them, as if she knew in her bones that everything was transient. Even people.

I turned to the bathroom door behind me, still as I'd left it. "Give me tonight to talk to him," I said. "It would give you time to pack, and I could be back by morning."

She averted her eyes with a shallow inhale, looking for a moment like she might lose her nerve.

"What is it?"

"Nothing." She flashed me a reassuring smile. The biggest smile I'd ever seen on her. "We'll leave in the morning, then?"

"First thing." I rose to my feet, handing her the towel sitting on the sink.

"Uh." I was halfway out the bathroom door when I halted, turning around with a grin. "How do you feel about cats?"

Vertical Victory
Corbie, France, November 1918

Wiggling the pencil between my thumb and index finger, I tapped it against the bed. The words wouldn't come. Every groan or staccato click of the nurse's heels was an excuse to lift my eyes from the unfinished letter, just long enough blind myself with the window light bouncing off the white tile floors.

Things were swell. I was alive. Indestructible, in fact.

"Good morning. How are we feeling today?"

Dropping my arm next to the other crumpled attempts, I looked up to greet the friendly voice at my bedside with a smile. "Like a horse piss, Marie."

"Vertical victory."

That was her tagline. Her way of reminding me that I was still standing. She'd said it when I first awoke in the influenza ward, drowning in phlegm and mentally preparing myself for my meeting with the grim reaper—and every day since.

She reached to check my vitals, shifting her tone. "How are you holding up, honey?"

I looked down at the name etched across the letter in my lap, bringing my thumb to my bottom lip. "Fine," I mumbled.

I could feel her eyes on me, tracing my face like a concerned mother hen. She hadn't forgotten how she'd found me a week ago, soaking my pillow with tears in the middle of the night.

Hail Mary, full of grace, the Lord is with thee, she'd recited quietly, taking a seat on my bed. *Holy Mary, mother of God, so stricken with grief, help us to bear our own suffering.*

"And how are you today?" I asked, sitting up so she could reach my bandage.

"I'm happy to see you're getting some color back," she replied, unrolling a fresh strip of gauze. "You've got a visitor this morning."

"A visitor?" I choked. Some notice would've been nice.

"You've been asking for him." I'd hardly uttered his name before she turned to Dane, standing in the doorway. "He's still weak from the pneumonia, but the worst is over," she said as he walked over to join us.

He hovered for a moment. I could only imagine how rough I looked to him, unbathed and tangled in the linen bedsheets. Last time he'd seen me, I'd still been in school. God, we'd been young.

"He has nine lives, your brother," said Marie, seeing herself out.

"Not a bad place to be laid up," he remarked, taking a seat on the stool next to me. "Seems like a nice town."

"The walls of the hospital are really scenic."

He scanned the blank room of the ward. "Good to know you still have your humor."

"I didn't know you were coming. I would've—"

"You don't need to clean up for me." There was pain in his voice as he spoke, as if I'd implied that we were strangers now.

"I know," I added. "But I at least would've put on a shirt."

Dane—whose only response to my plans to enlist had been a short letter that read, *do not come to Europe*—stood up and leaned over, offering the most tender of hugs. "It's good to see you," he said quietly over my shoulder. "I'm sorry I couldn't come sooner."

"It's good to see you, too," I replied, trying to suppress the urge to cough as he pulled away.

"How are you?"

I shrugged. "*Vertical victory.* Well...almost."

"Keeping yourself entertained, I see," he remarked, motioning to the letter next to my hand. "Dora?"

I turned the page over. "Do you remember Charlie Beckham from my letters?"

Dropping his brows, he narrowed his eyes on the edge of my bed. "Your nurse told me what happened."

"Dora was his fiancée. They were supposed to marry when he got back."

"I'm sure hearing from one of his friends will be a comfort to her."

I picked up the paper again, folding it in half. "I can't bear to write the words."

"No," he agreed. "What's there to say?"

Between the two of us, it was hard to say who'd seen more carnage. But while Dane had been faithfully driving ambulances in Italy, I'd been in France, leading men my own age to an early grave. In that respect, we *were* strangers.

"Is the Red Cross finished, then?" I asked finally. "Now that Germany surrendered?"

"As far as I'm concerned, it is."

I nodded, grabbing the chestnut box that sat atop my bedside table. "I was discharged a week ago," I said, nudging him to take it.

"What's this?"

"A parting gift."

A WEEK EARLIER————————

Marie told me he'd died around sunrise, without ever seeing the calico skies and sunshine of that brillant November morning.

I greeted her with eager eyes, itching for information the moment she appeared at my bedside. "Anything for me?"

"Afraid not—hold still for me, now."

I winced as the bloodied gauze stuck to my skin. "No word from Lucille?"

"I haven't seen her yet."

"When do you think you will?"

"When I have a spare second," she scolded. "It's a busy morning, you know. Everyone is shuffling about, trying to make sure everything's in order. Speaking of which—" She rolled her cart closer to the edge of my bed.

"Christ almighty," I sneered, spotting the shaving kit. "What's the occasion?"

Her face soured as she reached for the brush.

"Ah, right," I replied, suddenly remembering. "That's today."

Marie tilted my chin and began to apply the cream to my patchy cheeks.

"It'll be nice to feel human again at least," I murmured, lifting my eyes to the ceiling.

"I trust you're looking forward to receiving your medal?" The question felt sharper than the blade against my jawline, but thankfully I was saved from having to formulate an answer she would deem appropriate. "I think it's nice they're bringing them here," she added.

"It would've been better to attend the ceremony."

"Now, there are a lot of boys who didn't make it to that Armistice ceremony."

Didn't I fucking know it—though she'd meant the doughboys in the hospital, not the countless dead.

"So no word on Beckham at all?" I prodded. "I'm not contagious anymore, so I should be able to see him soon, right?"

He'd arrived at the hospital only a week after me with a bad case of *the runs*, and as dumb luck would have it, his nurse just so happened to be friends with Marie. The day I received my first letter from downstairs, my fever finally broke. Like dutiful aunties, our nurses had indulged us for nearly two weeks, passing notes back and forth from the influenza ward.

"Maybe next week, if you play your cards right," she promised.

"The sooner I can see him myself, the sooner I'll stop pestering you for correspondence." I grinned persuasively.

Marie grabbed the towel, cleaning the edge of the blade. "I'll tell you what," she said, wiping my face clean. "You focus on your visit this morning, and I'll go downstairs and talk to Lucille."

"You've got a deal, Marie."

"There we are," she said, handing me a mirror. "Remember him?"

I squinted at myself. My face had aged a hundred years.

"You look very handsome."

"And you sound like my mother," I teased, returning the mirror.

Marie rose to her feet, patting my shoulder endearingly. "She would be very proud of you today."

I looked up, meeting the glimmer in her cornflower blue eyes with a meek smile.

"I'll be back," she whispered cheerfully.

I reached up to touch my cleanly shaven face as I watched her pass under the ticking clock.

10:10 a.m.

They were set to arrive in twenty minutes, and hopefully for my sake, they'd distribute the medals by wing. Otherwise, I'd be toward the end, and I'd have rather liked to get it over with. I was more interested in hearing from Beckham—likely downstairs scribbling away on paper, describing his dysentery with the sort of detail I could do without—than I was in receiving superiors in shiny buttons. Though admittedly, the vainer side of me wondered what a medal would look like pinned to my uniform. Or what they'd say about it back home, whenever I got there.

A week from now, I would lay it on the table face up, next to our game of rummy and glasses of orange juice, and Beckham would say *at least you have something to show for it, Thom*. Just Beckham and me. The last of us.

"...And here you'll find the second wing."

My eyes snapped upward to meet the voice.

"Do watch your step, Colonel," the nurse continued. "The floors are still a little wet."

"I guess the war is really over."

I looked to the bed next to me. My neighbor, who'd never so much as uttered a word to me, gawked at the group of officers. I slid backward, through my fuzzy recollections of damp bedsheets and fever dreams, to the triumphant shouts of November 11th. To the tear-streaked cheeks of our nurses, who laughed uncontrollably as they huddled like pigeons.

"Yeah," I added. "I guess it is."

"Are you getting anything?"

"Nothing special," I lied.

Marie had told me I was set to receive a Distinguished Service Cross for Ypres, but mentioning it to a guy with a punctured lung would've felt too much like bragging. He'd see soon enough.

We watched with intrigue as the colonel handed a box to an infantryman, saying something I couldn't quite make out before moving down the line toward us. I looked left just in time to see Marie appear at the top of the staircase, and running on the exhausted fumes of high hopes, I immediately perked up.

"Holden Thompson? 27th division?"

"Yes," I replied, eyes still on my nurse.

"I'm Colonel Daniel Devore, and this is..."

I focused ahead, through his words and introductions, fixating on the crumpled white between Marie's fingers. Not a letter—but a *tissue* to accompany weepy, avoidant eyes. A coldness came over me as she rushed past the officers without a word, a familiar madness I'd grown accustomed to. The unrelenting reminder that I was alone, and nothing was holy.

"...on behalf of the United States Army, we'd like to issue—"

"Penny for my sacrifices?" I asked, finally meeting the eye of the colonel.

He frowned at my derogatory remark.

"To thank you for your sacrifices," the Major next to him chimed in. *"Captain."*

"Keep your thanks."

The ward grew silent enough to hear the cricket chirping in the corner.

"Give me a minute here," the colonel ordered quietly.

Looking hesitant, the clerk between them dabbed his forehead with the black of his sleeve before passing him the box. Sliding it onto my bedside table, the colonel took a seat beside me as the others continued. His expression was grim. Hardened.

"Spare a cigarette, Colonel?" I asked.

He reached into his pocket, shuffling the pack until a cigarette came forward. I grabbed it with two fingers and tucked it in between my lips.

He leaned over to light it. "Where are you from?"

"Virginia."

"I've thought about retiring just south of D.C. when this is all over and done with," he replied. "The world just keeps getting smaller."

I coughed halfway through my inhale like it was my first smoke. "It'll never be over."

"Listen, kid." He let out a deep, exhausted sigh. "Take it from me. It doesn't ever get any easier. Losing people."

People. That's all they were now—nameless statistics, too many to count.

"It never…"

"I want out."

"All right," he replied, adjusting himself in the chair. "And what then? Once you're out?"

I stared at the cigarette between my fingers, until the string of smoke began to blur with tears that wouldn't fall.

"I'll tell you."

I turned to see him eyeing me with intent familiarity, like he was talking to a younger version of himself.

"Find a girl and settle down. Start a family. Forget about all of this." I watched as his brow furrowed over his hazel eyes that had seen too much. "The same thing that kept you alive—your anger and resentment. It'll kill you now, if you let it."

I placed the cigarette back in my mouth limply, dropping my eyes to my lap.

"Take the medal, kid," he added, rising to his feet. "They don't give these to just anybody."

"Colonel—"

He halted, turning back to see me twirling the cigarette anxiously between my fingers.

"What did you say your name was, again?"

"Devore."

I nodded. "I'll remember that."

The colonel passed by Marie, who approached me with tearful eyes, clutching both hands in front of her.

"I'll put it out," I said, holding the cigarette away.

Next thing I knew, she was sitting on the edge of my bed, rocking me in her arms as if I were her own son. "Honey…your friend, he…"

"I know, Marie." I laid my cheek weakly on her shoulder. "I know."

Dane's eyes widened when I pulled the gold cross out of the box, dangling it between us by its royal blue ribbon. I laid it face up in my palm, showcasing the bleeding patriotism against the spotty window light as he observed with a cautious silence. I would've wondered what I'd done to earn it, too, if I were him.

"How much do you think it would weigh?" I asked absently. "On the scales of Osiris."

Dane laced his hands, bringing the cluster of fingers to his chin in contemplation as he sat on the stool next to me.

"It's much heavier than a human heart," I replied, dropping it back into the box.

"What do you think about staying on for a while?" he asked suddenly.

I squinted up at him. "What do you mean?"

"I'm headed back to Paris. I've got a flat lined up for the next twelve months."

"What would I do in Paris?"

"Drink wine. Learn French."

I folded the ribbon, tucking it delicately alongside my victory medal and Rick's pendant necklace.

"It would give you a chance to decompress…until you figure things out," he added. "Unless you had other plans."

Up until this point, I'd been convinced I wouldn't make it to twenty-five. So, no, I didn't. "Okay." I sat up in bed, crossing my arms. "Yeah, okay."

"Leaving me so soon?" Marie teased, suddenly reappearing.

I looked apprehensively between them, then focused on her. "Do you think I'll do okay? Out there?"

She smiled reassuringly, setting a pile of folded clothes at the end of my bed. "I think you'll do splendid."

That afternoon, I walked out of the hospital with nothing to my name but a small suitcase of Army essentials, a broken typewriter, and a tattered, war-torn body. But I was free.

"Jesus, it's cold." I shivered in my loose uniform, draping my arm over Dane's shoulder.

"It's November," he reminded, helping me shift my weight. "Are you okay?"

Of course, Dane wanted the comfortable answer. Peering through the sunshine, I looked out to the iron gate strung with a hospital flag as I stood on the stoop. I'd been naïve to think that the six of us would make it out unscathed, but I couldn't have fathomed being the only one.

"Holden?"

"I'm great," I assured, grinning at a young nurse as she climbed the stairs. "Paris, here we come."

At Both Ends
Paris, January 23, 1919 cont.

Lady was waiting under the stairwell when I opened the door to our flat for the last time. "Miss me?" I asked, running my fingers over her arched back. I took a knee to the tile floor, gazing up to our apartment. The foyer felt damp, and the smell of winter lingered like unfinished business. I'd left Vanina's feeling confident, but my nerve had evaporated with the smoke of each cigarette I'd inhaled on the way. I didn't need anyone to tell me I was making a rash decision. I already knew.

Scurrying up the stairs ahead of me, Lady waited patiently by the door as I pulled out my key.

"Dane?" I called.

The cat bolted through the crack and into the vacant room, where an oil and canvas sat propped on the desk next to a few paintbrushes dunked in opaque water. The room felt recently inhabited, like I'd just missed him.

"Where'd he run off to?" I asked, examining the painting closer. I could only assume the scene had been painted from his imagination, but something about it looked familiar, as if he'd plucked the charming freshwater brook from my own private memory bank.

I was roused from my meditation by the sound of Lady

jumping up on the kitchen table, followed by a cascade of rustling paper. She didn't bother to hide her satisfaction when I turned around, standing proudly on the table overlooking the mail she'd knocked onto the floor.

"Was that really necessary?" I knelt down, gathering the several letters she'd sent flying. "*And* nothing for me," I muttered, shuffling through them. I stopped, caught on the return address of an open envelope. "Or maybe…" I added, reaching inside.

"Dear Dane, thank you for keeping me updated on Holden." Seeing my name written out made me wince. "If you think he would do better back home, you're under no obligation to look after him. It would be unfair of us to ask that when he's *not being honest with you?*" The walls felt like they were shrinking inward, but I couldn't stop.

I'd just flipped to the back when the front door opened, and in walked Dane, as well as the reason he'd left in such a hurry—all dressed to impress in her crimson lips and floral coat. It was clear from the way he reached for her hand that he thought they were alone.

"Well then," I said. "I guess it's a party."

Camille whipped around with my name on her lips, but she didn't dare speak it, as tongue-tied as Dane to see me standing there. And just like that, I was struck by Cupid's arrow. It had happened right under my nose, a brilliant flicker of serendipity.

I loved her.

"There you are," she whispered at last.

"Where have you been?" asked Dane.

My eyes flickered over to my brother, remembering the letter clutched behind my back. "Do you mind?"

Camille turned to Dane. "It's okay. I want to talk to him," she assured.

He nodded submissively, glancing at me once before reaching for the door and seeing himself out.

Once we were alone, I set my sights back on Camille. "You were looking for me?"

"Everywhere," she admitted, wringing her hands. "Then Dane told me he hadn't seen you, and didn't know when you'd be back."

I rolled my eyes. "Oh—did he, now."

Dropping her lashes, she smiled, seemingly amused by my evident jealousy.

"Why, then?" I asked.

"I saw the state you were in when you left. The way you looked at me. I..." She burrowed her nose in the crevice of my collar bone as I hugged her to me, sealing my affections with a kiss to her forehead. "I was quick to judge," she said, sighing. "I was angry."

"It was founded."

"But it was before you really got to know me, like you said."

I squeezed her close, resting my jaw on the top of her head. Sooner or later, she'd realize I was still in my clothes from last night. She'd ask where I'd been.

"The past is past," she added.

I closed my eyes, feeling her fingers dig into my back as she hugged me tighter. *God*, I didn't want to tell her. I wanted to go back and freeze the clock, come home, be sleeping in my own bed when she came knocking in the morning.

"What is it? Aren't you happy to see me?"

"Yes," I whispered, wanting to cry. "So happy."

She grazed her fingers over my cheekbone, kissing my mute lips. I could see the trepidation in her eyes as she pulled away, searching my face for whatever was wrong.

"I was with someone last night."

"You...what?"

The words wouldn't come a second time.

"You were with Jeanne."

"No. Someone else."

She released herself from me, stumbling backward.

"We made plans to go north together," I confessed. "I didn't want to lie to you!"

"I can't believe I..." She let out a pitiful laugh. "Have I stroked your ego enough for one day?"

"I thought if I couldn't have a *happy* ending, I might at least have a content one! If I'd known you'd be standing here this morning—"

"Then what!"

I paused.

"*What,* Holden?" she demanded. "Go on, say it!"

"I wouldn't have gone there!"

"You never wanted to be with me—you just want to be with *someone*—anyone will do! Just as long as you don't have to be alone with yourself."

"I..." I bit my lip. "You don't think that my feelings for you were genuine?"

"It took you exactly an hour to jump in bed with someone else!"

"You broke my heart last night."

"I suppose it's a good thing you had someone lined up to make you feel better, then," she replied, turning her back to me.

"It didn't even help," I added weakly. "I thought only of you."

"That's a cruel thing to say." She walked over to the mattress, hugging her knees as she took a seat on its edge. "You're as capable of love as you are of remorse." Camille outstretched her hand to the cowering kitten under the desk, and I watched from the windowsill with a sorry heart as Lady crawled out and began brushing her tail against her shins. "You tried to tell me when we met," she said, bringing the cat onto her lap, "that I wouldn't like what I found."

"And you said you saw a light in me."

"I still do." She moved Lady onto the mattress, rising to her feet. "But it's the light of a candle burning at both ends."

I averted my eyes to a pair of doves sitting on the adjacent rooftop, unable to watch her leave.

"Camille."

She turned back to look at me with one hand on the rickety doorknob.

"I'll miss you," I said quietly.

"I'll miss you, too."

When I looked back to the window, the doves were gone.

"What happened?" Dane asked, sliding through the half open door. "She seemed upset."

"Why don't you chase after her and ask?" I countered, throwing my suitcase onto the mattress.

"It's not my fault you weren't here when she came by."

"No—" I glanced over my shoulder, cocking an eyebrow. "But convenient for you, nonetheless."

"*Convenient?* What about you—out all night with whoever else! The things you do to people who love you."

I laughed silently to myself, shoving clothes furiously into my suitcase. "She doesn't love me."

"What are you doing?" he asked.

"Getting out of your hair."

"What are you talking about?"

I grabbed the letter from my back pocket, crumpling it and tossing it at his feet. "You're a hypocrite."

He stammered, blinded by the spotlight I'd thrown on him. "It's out of context. I wrote to him about your shellshock."

"And you thought it was your place to tell them about that, not mine."

"*I'm* the one who has to sit here, day in and day out, watching you self-destruct like Grandaddy—"

I slammed the suitcase shut, pointing my finger in warning. "Don't."

"Open your eyes, Holden. For once in your life."

"I'm going north, and I'm taking the cat. You can write the whole damn family about it for all I care."

"Running off with someone you don't even know? Great idea."

"I'm sure as hell not asking for your blessing," I said, grabbing the suitcase by the handle. "God knows you never asked for mine."

"I needed a fresh start, to get out on my own—it's hardly the same thing."

"Things got hard and you ran away," I spat. "Where do you think I learned it from?"

Now he was angry. "I told you not to come here—I tried to help you. All I try to do is help you, but God forbid you see outside of your own experience for more than two minutes," he countered. "You're not the only person who's suffered from this war, and I think it's about time someone told you that."

"You don't know what I've suffered," I said, shoving past him with my suitcase.

"How would I?" he shouted. "When you don't trust me enough to tell me?"

"Because you're not ready to hear it," I murmured, grabbing the Royal. "Don't ask questions you don't want the answer to."

"What a martyr you are."

I let out a sigh, turning to face him as I stood at the door. "Fine. You want to know the reason I came to France—that the reason I left school was because I was preyed on and exploited by someone I admired—is that what you want to hear, Dane?"

I may as well have hit him with a brick.

"*Good ole Frank,*" I added, revolted by the flavor his name left in my mouth. "Everything I know, I learned from him."

I waited for Dane to say something—*anything*—expectantly hanging on any possible word, but his silence was deafening.

"And now you're looking at me exactly how I imagined you would."

He inhaled shallowly, trying to steady his voice. "When?"

Shifting the Royal in my arm, I nudged my shoulder through the doorway. "When you were in Italy."

IN THE WINTER
VIRGINIA, MARCH 1909

I SHIVERED, peering through the rain droplets on the drafty window to the back of the car stacked with suitcases. Even the sprouting flowers along the walkway had been hit with an early spring frost, as if Mother Nature had determined that nothing should survive that winter.

I glanced over my shoulder from my seat on the windowsill, following a soft knock on my bedroom door. "What?"

Marceline peeked her nose through the crack.

"What is it?"

"Dorthia came by with her mom."

"Oh," I said, turning my attention back to the glass.

"They brought a pie," she went on, lowering her voice. "For Grandaddy."

I listened as she opened the door and tiptoed inside, though her footsteps were quiet as a mouse.

"I thought you might want to know she came by," she added.

I shrugged, pulling my knees to my chest. I could feel her disappointed stare burning a hole through my back, as if she'd been sure the visit from the girl down the street would pique my interest.

"It's a cherry pie. Your favorite. I'm sure Mama would let us cut it before—"

"I'm not hungry."

"Well, do you want to play a game? Jamie and I were just—"

"No, Marcie."

She sighed. "Okay."

Perching on the windowsill next to me, she joined in watching the scene below. Underneath the trunk of the car, Pop mouthed something to Dane. Maybe it was something about me.

"Dorthia said she was sorry for missing the funeral," Marceline added. "They've been on the eastern shore."

Dane looked back at him, nodding intently. More than likely, he'd only asked if he was sure he wasn't forgetting anything.

I scanned my palms, then raised my eyes to see Marceline awaiting a response. "Sorry. What?"

"New York's not so far, you know," she assured, combing her blush locks with her fingers.

"I'm fine, Marcie. I have a whole room to myself now." I motioned dramatically to the deserted left side of our previously shared bedroom.

She'd just opened her mouth to speak when a second knock at the door interrupted her.

Jamie peeked inside. "Did you ask about the pie?"

Marceline shot him a look. Her eyes screamed at him to *go away*—that him barging in was not part of the operation to pry me from my room.

"Well, does he want any?" Jamie asked.

"I'm not hungry," I said again.

"But it's—"

"Cherry. *I know.*"

Jamie frowned, looking like a pouting doll with his blue eyes and blond curls. "We're cutting it before Dane leaves. Mama said it would be a nice send off."

"Go back downstairs," Marceline shooed.

"Both of you," I added, turning to her.

"Me?" she huffed. "Why me?"

"Because," I replied, turning back to the window, "I want to be alone."

"He wants to sit in here and mope all day," Jamie teased.

Grabbing the book nearest to me, I launched it at him as he hung on my doorknob. *"Get out,"* I ordered.

"Ow!!"

Marceline stood abruptly, almost tripping over her skirt. "You know," she huffed, crossing her arms. "You don't have to be so mean."

"What are you talking about?"

"I was just trying to make you feel better!"

"You're doing that thing again," I grumbled. "That thing you always do where—"

"What thi—"

"Where you try to fix everything!" I shouted, throwing my hands in the air. "Pie isn't going to raise Grandaddy from the dead and it's not going to keep Dane from leaving, either."

Flipping her hair over her shoulder, she walked to the door. "I don't know why I bother," she added, closing it behind her.

The trunk of the car shut on the other side of the window, filling my ears with a silent finality. I looked down at my palm, focusing on the self-inflicted incision in the center. It had healed into an almost star-shaped scar, unnoticeable to anyone but me.

THREE WEEKS PRIOR————————

"I don't want to grow old," I'd said, ripping my pocketknife from the bark of the old oak with numb fingers.

"He died because he wouldn't stop drinking. Not because he was old."

"How do you know that?" I countered.

Dane was quiet as he sat against the water's edge, jabbing its partially frozen rapids with a stick. From my place on the bank, it looked like a scene out of Whitman's most somber poem—

skeleton branches and withered honeysuckle vines being the only remnants of our summer meadow, and us, dressed in our best black. We hadn't exchanged a single word as we crunched through the dead leaves to the winding brook, managing to skirt the post service sympathies by slipping out the door unnoticed.

"It doesn't matter anyway," I added, wiping the blade with my finger. "It didn't even look like him in the casket."

"I was afraid of that."

I paused, lowering my aim. "Is that why you didn't look?"

"Yeah."

I squinted ahead, turning back to my target to concentrate. "I wish I hadn't," I muttered, chucking the knife.

"I wish I had." Dane looked over his shoulder, grinning at me ironically.

I grabbed the knife, blowing off the splinters. "What do you think about it? About *God's plan?*"

"I think Pop should've been a preacher."

"I'm serious," I pressed, gazing upward at the wood line. Birds sat perched in the branches above the icy stream. Among them, a bluebird.

Dane rose to his feet, swiping a rock from the ground. "It's a nice thought," he added. "Better than the alternative."

"That everything is random?"

"That everything is random," he repeated back, spacing out the words like the rock he skipped across the water. "Nothing seems crueler than that."

Dragging my feet, I joined him at the edge of the brook. "What about her?"

"You mean—"

"Yeah," I said, picking up my own rock. "Your mother."

Dane thought to himself, then spoke rather frankly. "If she hadn't died, you wouldn't be here."

I peered down at my reflection through the jagged edges of the watery mirror.

"And that's not to say that it's right or that I'm glad," he said, slinging his arm around my shoulder. "But for what it's worth, I can't imagine my life otherwise."

A leaf fell, erasing my grin as it casted ripples across the water. Dane grew quiet, as if he were thinking. "You know how we've talked about going to New York?" he asked finally.

I looked up at him, eyebrows raised in anticipation.

"And how there are more opportunities for artists there?"

"And writers, too." I tossed my rock, watching it sink to the bottom on the first skip. "What about it?"

He walked over to a nearby log, taking a seat with a shallow exhale. "I wanted to talk to you about it first," he said, lacing his fingers. "I've been mulling it over the last few months, but then everything happened with Grandaddy…"

I clenched my jaw, focusing carefully on digging the dirt from beneath my thumbnail with the tip of my knife as he went on.

"It's just that I'm eighteen now, and I—"

"You want to go by yourself."

"Well, I'm not a kid anymore."

"And I am?"

"That's not what I said."

Glancing upward, I looked to the bluebird in the tree, ever watchful.

"It may not be such a bad thing for you either," he went on. "And by the time you finish school, I'll be established and have my own place, and you can come stay with me."

I took a seat beside him, tracing the blade with my finger delicately.

"Say something, Holden."

"I'm happy for you."

"I promise you'll understand when you're older."

My eyes flickered over him, back to the dull meadow's branches.

"What do you keep looking at?" He turned over his shoulder. "Oh—that's bizarre," he added, spotting the vibrant blue feathers of the bird.

"Grandaddy always said they were special."

Dane turned back to face me. "It's early to be seeing bluebirds. They usually don't come around until—"

"Promise to write," I interrupted. "If you go to New York."

"Of course, I'll write."

"I mean *really* write," I pressed. "I don't want to miss anything."

With a smile, he motioned for my knife. I winced, watching as he opened his right palm and dug the point into the center.

"I promise to write every week if you do," he pledged, flipping the blade around. "In the summer and in the winter."

I grabbed the handle, pressing the blade into the middle of my opposite hand with a satisfied smirk. "In the summer and in the winter," I repeated.

"All right, then," he'd said, extending his hand for a shake. "It's settled."

I was staring solemnly into the overcast sky, lost somewhere between our midsummer strolls and blood pacts, when I heard a third knock at the door.

"I said I'm not hungry."

"Are you sure?"

Dane walked over and sat down on the windowsill, sliding me a decadent slice of cherry pie on a piece of Ma's china. I looked at him expectantly.

"It's almost time."

"It'd be a shame if you missed your train," I sneered.

"I thought maybe if I brought you pie, I could bribe you into seeing me off," he murmured, tapping on the glassy window.

"You don't have to bribe me," I replied, reluctantly picking up the plate. "I was just waiting for you to ask."

Dane chuckled to himself. His gaze followed the window up

to the ceiling, then to our wallpapered walls. "I'll miss this. This view. The yard…"

"The bird watching," I added, cutting the tip of the pie with my fork. "In the spring."

"And the stars at night."

I smiled around a mouthful of cherries. "Neighbors who bring pie."

"You marking up my books."

"Having your books to steal."

He gazed with wistful eyes to the loaded car below the window, then looked up at me with a reassuring grin. "It'll be like I never left."

A Thousand Things
Paris, January 23, 1919 cont.

I tucked my chin against Lady, nestled comfortably in my coat collar. "Well, that couldn't have gone better," I mumbled.

No. My secret spurting from my mouth like the blood of a punctured artery had not been part of the plan. In a perfect world, I would've spared my brother the burden and taken it to my grave; just me and it, cradling each other in my casket for all eternity, and his perception of me—still intact.

The noon bells rang throughout the city, scattering the pigeons from their watchtowers onto the groups of loitering Parisians. I filed it away—the spinning accents, dive cafes and the ever-present smell of garbage—as I trudged through the street with everything I owned, knowing that, despite it all, a part of me would miss Paris when I was gone. I kissed the top of Lady's head, clutching her to my chest.

Vanina's duplex stood between two taller buildings, which cast a midday shadow as we made our approach. I slowed my step, struck by the home's apparent emptiness. There were no lights on inside, no hint of life beyond the door.

She was gone.

Dropping my luggage at my feet, I stepped onto her stoop and reached for the twice-folded note caught in the door.

. . .

Holden,
 A thousand things.

"Le beau charmeur."

I squinted upward to see Miss Helene perched on the neighboring stoop, wearing an unforgiving scorn. "Sorry," I said, dropping the note to my side. "I don't speak—"

"Look who decided to drop by in the daytime," she said in English. "I've seen you around here, causing all sorts of trouble for that girl."

"I think you have me mistaken."

The old woman chuckled without humor, resting her weight on the broomstick she held. "Yours isn't a face I'd soon forget."

I eyed her, reaching for the cigarette I'd tucked in my ear.

"Don't you want to know where they went?"

I struck a match to light the cherry. "I don't think she wants to be found," I countered with a puff of smoke. "And I can't imagine you'd want to tell me."

"It's a shame. A father who takes no interest in his own child."

"I'm not Emma's father."

"I'm not talking about *Emma*. I'm talking about the baby."

"The baby," I echoed.

"Oh—don't pretend you didn't know! It's obvious to anyone with eyes, as delicate as she's been lately."

I reached for my suitcase, meeting her stone-cold stare. "It's not mine. It couldn't be."

"No, of course it isn't." She scoffed, shaking her head. "You're a sorry excuse for a man. A coward."

I nodded, flicking the butt to the ground. "Don't I know it." Adjusting the strap on my shoulder, I turned off the stoop and made my way back down the street.

There were no displaced soldiers or Romani elders there to greet me when I opened the door to Saint-Étienne-du-Mont. Just Lady and me. Steeped in quiet, the palatial walls dripped with orphic tranquility as I found my way down the aisle and took a seat in the front row. Running off with Vanina had been visionary at best and a last-ditch effort at worst, but even so. The only plan I had left was as slain as the crucifix peering down on us from the double-spiral staircase.

I'd been sitting for hours, meditating on the tide of the lamented when I heard the sanctuary doors open behind me, followed by footsteps. Without a word, Dane joined the sulking choir of one, taking the seat next to me.

I lifted my watery eyes to the softened glow of the votive candles. "How'd you know where to find me?"

"The most unexpected place is the best place to hide." He cleared his throat as we sat shoulder to shoulder, maintaining our collective gaze forward. "Though, some might argue that you're suspiciously agnostic these days."

"For all my quarrels with God, I've never claimed he didn't have a sense of humor," I said. "You were right about her."

"Holden…"

"Don't," I whispered, afraid of the words that might follow. "Please. If there's one thing I can't take, it's your pity."

I'd never once witnessed my brother cry. Not when he left home, not over his dead mother—never once, until I finally looked over, and saw the reflection of tear streaks on his cheek. In a reversal of roles, I reached my arm around his shoulders, bringing him in close.

"I tried to tell you." I glanced down at Lady, who purred against my chest. "That no one really wants the truth."

"I can't believe I didn't see it."

"I hid it well. I never wanted to give anyone a reason to wonder."

"Wonder what?"

"If I'd brought it on myself."

"You didn't," he said. "I know that much."

I could sense the tension raging inside of him. Whether to ask for the details, whether or not he even wanted to hear them.

"It was one time. He came onto me at his house, offered to publish me. I didn't really know what…" The words caught in my throat.

"So you stopped writing."

I nodded. "He has a piece of me I can never get back. It was easier not to try."

"If I would've been home more—"

"Don't." I inhaled sharply, wetting my lips. "It's done and over with."

"Nothing that happens to us is ever done and over with."

"I know it," I urged. "But promise me that this dies here."

Dane sat up, folding his hands in prayer formation. "All right," he said, offering one.

I grabbed on, realigning our scars.

He brought his eyes to mine, shaking hard. "It dies here."

We sat in comfortable silence together for a long time afterward, watching the sanctuary darken as the luminaries traded places in the sky.

"She would've been better off with you," I admitted. "Camille." I slipped my hand into my pants pocket, catching my finger on the chain as I felt around for the Saint Stephen pendant. "Everyone who involves themselves with me ends up regretting it."

"If you're meaning the letter, you weren't supposed to find out that way. I was going to talk to you about it."

"Do you think it would help?" I asked, staring up at the crucifix. "Going back home?"

His eyes followed the room, looking across to the quiet illumination of the shrine.

"I know you're just trying to do right by me," I added. "You always have."

"Well," he said finally. "You know what Paris holds for you. At least right now."

"What if nothing is the same when I get back?"

"I don't imagine it would be." He paused, smiling weakly at me. "But you never know what's around the corner."

Letter from Marceline
March 12, 1919

Dear Holden,

I was thrilled to receive your letter, and even more thrilled to hear about your plans to return home. The end of April, you said? I can hardly wait. Jamie and I were starting to think you may never come home, though, who could blame you?

Paris sounds like it's been a thrilling adventure from the way you've described it, and I fear you may be bored here—but as you said in your last letter, 'who knows what's just around the corner?' There is life to be lived still, in our cozy little town. I pray it's what you need right now.

Work is busy, despite the influenza, and I know Papa would love to have you back. He's remarked on possibly renting the upstairs apartment of the shop since it's just sitting anyway, but I'm sure he'd let you stay there until you get on your feet. Oh, I can't wait until you get here! I hope things open up by then.

Jamie is well. He's been in Richmond helping with hospital overflow, and he's quite proud of that fact, though it's a shame he had to do it at all. I don't know if you remember Dorthia Murphy from down the street, but she passed away last week from a terrible case. Mama and I took them a ham, but we had to leave it on the porch. Death is such a lonely and persistent thing, but enough about that.

It makes complete sense that you would want to stay in Paris a bit longer to tie up loose ends. I hope whatever—or *whomever*—they are, that you can embellish the details and remember them fondly.

With love,
    Marcie

Just Between Us
Paris, April 25, 1919

I stepped out of the taxi and onto the curb, running my fingers through my damp hair in a final attempt to tame it.

"You behave yourself, now," said Dane.

I looked inside, past the piled suitcases in the middle, to see him holding Lady up from under her arms.

He leaned over the barricade. "Good luck," he said, passing her off to me.

I nodded at my reflection in the window, tapping the side of the car swiftly. "I won't be long."

It felt as though I had strolled into one of his paintings—as if I'd been painted into the layered brushstrokes of an upper-class neighborhood in bloom. Cat in one hand and fiddling my pocket pendant with the other, I made my way down the bustling sidewalk with my sight set on the lush house, vignetted in blooming rose-tangled trellises.

"Here goes nothing," I mumbled, taking a knee.

Lady jumped down onto the stone walkway, next to a small patch of yellow wildflowers lining its edge. I leaned over to examine their dusty petals, plucking a few from the root. Rising to my feet, I straightened my tweed sport coat and glanced up to Camille's window. I wasn't sure who would answer the door when I knocked, but I had to knock. I clicked my tongue, coaxing Lady to follow me up the walkway, but I quickly lost her attention to a nearby grasshopper in the yard.

Clearing my throat, I loosened my shoulders and reached for the lion shaped door knocker.

"You're early!" I listened for her lighthearted laugh as she swung the door open. "I haven't even—"

I nodded hello, the flowers in my hand suddenly feeling as arbitrary as a stick of dynamite. No longer a youthful girl, she stood before me in a slim fitted powder, blue dress which hugged her thin frame. She would be somebody's wife.

"Hi, Camille."

She stepped outside and closed the door behind her, leaning back on it. "You're back."

"I never left." I shrugged. "It wasn't in the cards."

She had no visible reaction to my words, but her eyes were inquisitive as they watched me wipe my nervous brow with the back of my wrist. "Are you well?"

"I'm headed home," I said. "Back to the States."

Her eyes dropped to the flowers I held at my side. "I guess spring finally came."

I smirked, handing them off to her.

Camille giggled softly, examining the stems. "These things… they drive our gardener mad."

"Us, too." I thought backward—to the summer wind whipping my dark curls across my forehead, and me, gazing across the carnelian August horizon line, peppered with bodies and wildflowers which had no decency for the dead. When I finally looked up, Camille's expression had fallen, almost as if she'd seen it, too. "But you have to admit, their resilience is something to be admired," I added with a smile.

"When do you leave?" she asked, picking a petal and letting it drift to the ground.

"Well…" I motioned to the cab over my shoulder, waiting patiently on the corner. "I've got a four o'clock train to catch."

"You're on your way, then."

"I didn't want to leave without saying goodbye. I hope that's okay."

Lady charged out of the rustling boxwoods, running between us in hot pursuit of the grasshopper who'd been tempting her.

"I should've known your shadow would be close by." Camille knelt in front of me, extending her fingers to the kitten. "*My*, she's gotten big."

"And there's something else," I added, dropping to their level.

Her hand fell limp as she looked up at me in disbelief. "Holden, *no*," she protested. "You have to take her with you."

"I don't even know where I'm going to live when I get home… and Dane, well. You can never count on him sticking around anywhere for too long." I rose to my feet, brushing the cat hair off my pants. "Paris is her home."

Camille straightened up, leaving Lady at our feet. "But you love her."

"Very much," I replied, lifting my eyes to hers. "But I can't take her with me."

I could feel my heart strangling itself in the strands of her hair. I wanted to be the breeze brushing them across her parted lips, the sunshine on her skin.

"Then I'll take good care of her," she promised enthusiastically. "Don't you worry about that—I'll spoil her! She'll sunbathe in the windows and sleep on my pillow."

I leaned over to pet Lady, who weaved between my legs. "You really were my little smudge of good luck," I murmured, planting a kiss on my furry savior. "Thank you," I said, turning my attention back to Camille.

"Just between us," she added, "I'm glad I'll have something to remember you by."

"Me, too," I replied, forcing a grin.

"Well…I'd better not hold you up," she said, taking the cat into her arms.

"Right." I nodded, stepping back. I'd kept Dane waiting long enough. "Goodbye, Camille."

My head was spinning with a bittersweet high when I stepped down onto the walkway. Everything had gone to plan—better than I'd imagined, even. But the pounding in my chest was growing by the second, and the words were burning in my throat. With minutes to go, I spun around to see Camille closing the front door, locking Lady inside. Catching her mossy eyes from across the lawn, I smiled, then sprinted back to them.

"What are you doing?" she called, running into the grass to meet me.

I huffed, out of breath. "I couldn't leave without *really* saying goodbye—" I reached for the back of her neck, bringing her lips to mine, soft heartedly as a childhood sweetheart. "I learned some French for you," I whispered, pressing my cheek to her temple. *"Je t'aime,* Camille."

She pulled away, all smiles.

"Je t'aime," I said again, wrapping her in a final embrace. "Je' t'aime. Je t'aime."

"I love you, too," she whispered back, wiping the tears from under my eyes. "Au revoir, mon amour."

I dove into the backseat of the cab and slid across the leather seats, resting my arm overtop the barricade of luggage separating Dane and me.

"So…how'd it go?" he asked.

"From the look on his face, I'd say it went well."

I met the eyes of our driver, peering over his shoulder from the front seat.

"Well? Did you tell her goodbye?"

I looked down at my hands in my lap, grinning to myself.

"That's a yes."

"Are you ready?" Dane asked.

"I think so."

Gripping the back of the seat, I turned around and looked out the tiny back window as we pulled off the curb, catching a last glimpse of Camille closing the door behind her. *"Au revoir,* little dove," I whispered under my breath. There was hope for me, even if there would be none for us.

I sat back, shifting my attention to the scenes of fervent spring fever on the other side of the window. The breeze blew through the front, ruffling our hair in the backseat as we began to drive, and Dane drummed on the sun warmed leather shell of the suitcase.

"Do you ever feel like we've done this all before?" I mused, keeping my eyes on the cyan sky.

I looked over to see Dane eyeing me curiously. "Sure. Certain days, certain hours…"

"What do you think about it?"

"I'd say it means you're right where you're supposed to be."

"*God's plan*, you mean." I smiled cheekily as we rounded a corner, the Gare d'Austerlitz station coming into view. "I think we give far too much credit to God."

"Oh?" he pressed. "And who do you think we should we credit for this orchestrated chaos?"

"Ourselves," I replied confidently, twirling Rick's necklace in my pocket. "The human spirit and all its elasticity." I turned to Dane, waiting for him to tie my words neatly with a bow.

He met my eye with a twinkle. "How can you not write when you have so much to say?"

Epilogue

By Louisa M. Thompson Fredericksburg,
Virginia 1926

I TYPE this with a baby in my arm. The snowflakes outside the window have long turned to pear blossom petals, and my son—with his father's inherited temperament—quietly watches my fingers dance across the Royal's worn keys with steely eyes the color of a winter sea. Holden's photo sits in the keys of my typewriter for old times' sake. Nearby, the loose pages of his unknown memoir wait for resurrection.

They were the last thing I thought we'd stumble upon last December when I followed Marceline through the back door of the family tailoring shop, nine months pregnant and busting at the seams. Two-year-old Celia June stuck to my heels like glue, as if she were anticipating the arrival of her nameless playmate any second. In the end, it seemed to be Holden himself who suggested the name of his nephew.

I was in the back room when I noticed what looked to be a stack of papers sitting on the top shelf. Without thinking much of it, I grabbed onto the edge and pulled them down.

A chain dropped to my feet with a *clink*.

"Marceline!" I called, picking it up.

Peeking her head around the corner, she took a shallow breath, pointing to the stack of banded papers in my arm. "What is that?"

We stared dumbstruck at the handwriting, scribbled within the margins of the dusty, typed paper.

"This was with it," I said, passing off the necklace.

Marceline held the pendant to the lone, dimly lit bulb. "Saint Stephen."

I shifted the stack in my arm, flipping to the first page. "If you find yourself opening to this page, having stumbled across this written exorcism, I have only one real request," I read aloud. "Listen closely…"

Our eyes simultaneously snapped upward, finding each other.

"You are my priest, and I am your confessor."

I've spent the last six months in hibernation, binging my way —page by candlelit page—through a confessional story of a villainous hero, misguided lover and reluctant believer. As we always suspected, the magician in the glass castle wore many hats, and still, he shapeshifts.

We can only speculate why these words never made it to the burn pile. Perhaps Stephen knows.

For now, I will do with it only what I know Holden would want. I will give it a proper ending. Because a good story, *dear reader,* need never remain unfinished when there is another magician to pick up the pen.

Also by Elaine DeBohun
All the Yellow Posies

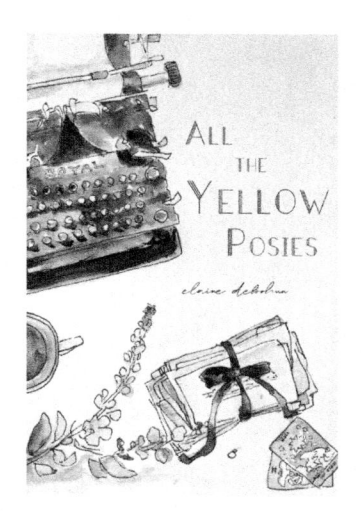

1919—the Great War has come to an end and small-town Fredericksburg, Virginia is still reeling from the last outbreak of 1918 influenza. Free-spirited Lou, an aspiring journalist from a wealthy family, answers the classified for an apartment above a local tailoring shop. There, she meets Holden Thompson—who's just returned from the Western Front. As she's brought further into his circle of family and friends, Lou quickly learns that, despite being charismatic, handsome and witty, Holden is tormented by the past. Unforeseen circumstances splinter the tight-knit group as they are carried into the roaring 20s—tied by tragedy and woven together by a thread of fate.

Acknowledgments

Like its sister book, *Stars on Fire* came as a surprise to me. Originally it was a *sequel* I had begun to write, until I received a nudge from a very adamant Holden, saying that if I was going to tell this story, I had to tell it from the beginning—that before we could watch these characters move forward, we had to go backward. So I shelved the project and took up this one instead. In the divinely-timed manner that is so often my life, my son was born in December of 2022. For this, I tip my hat to Mercury retrograde and say, "well played."

There are many people I'd like to thank for supporting me—Joey, Fran, Laura, Megan, my beta readers, my Holden lovers—but there are a couple I'd like to mention in depth. To Kathryne, undoubtedly my biggest cheerleader: thank you for your insight, for reading every draft and for listening to me brainstorm on Marco Polo for countless hours. If it weren't for you, *Stars on Fire* would've indeed been a novella. To Friel Black, my copyeditor: thank you for your encouragement, your love for my characters and your Gemini touch on this manuscript.

The cast of this novel is filled with names of deceased, whether it was me coming across names in old family letters or bearing witness to their passing during its gestation. It felt only appropriate to not only include them in this narrative but to acknowledge the honor it was to write them in—I like to think they had some influence over their cameos. For my grandaddy, Charlie Beckham, for whom I wrote a eulogy: I thought you would like that Holden uses your special toast. To Richard Spofford Lake, my mother's fiancé before I was born: we never met, but you've always felt like family to me. To my dear friend and former ARC reader, Meg: I wrote the scene of you and Henry shortly after we lost you. I think of you often. To the many other names mentioned —the family, the friends of friends and my two Pomeranians— thank you for playing a part in Holden's story.

And lastly, to Stephen Carter: thank you for the opening lines of Holden's prologue. The first thread of this tapestry started with you.

Printed in Great Britain
by Amazon